I0632448

Laurence Minot

Poems on Interesting Events in the Reign of King Edward III

Laurence Minot

Poems on Interesting Events in the Reign of King Edward III

ISBN/EAN: 9783744716161

Printed in Europe, USA, Canada, Australia, Japan

Cover: Foto ©Andreas Hilbeck / pixelio.de

More available books at **www.hansebooks.com**

POEMS

BY

LAURENCE MINOT.

POEMS

ON

INTERESTING EVENTS

IN THE REIGN OF

KING EDWARD III.

WRITTEN,

IN THE YEAR MCCCLII.

BY

LAURENCE MINOT.

WITH

A PREFACE, DISSERTATIONS, NOTES,

AND

A GLOSSARY.

LONDON:

PRINTED BY T. BENSLEY,

FOR T. EGERTON, WHITEHALL.

1795.

PREFACE.

THE neglect which writers of genius are occasionally condemned to experience, as well from their contemporaries as from posterity, was never exemplifyed, perhaps, in a more eminent degree than by the poet whofe works are now offered to the public. His very name appears totally unknown to Leland, Bale, Pitts, and Tanner: it is mentioned, in fhort, by no one writer, till late in the prefent century, nor is found to occur in any catalogue: while the filence of the public records would induce us to believe that the great monarch whom he has fo eloquently and earneftly panegyrifed was either ignorant of his existence or infenfible of his merit *.

That thefe equally elegant and fpirited compofitions were at length retrieved from the obfcurity in which they had been for ages intered was owing to a whimfical cir-cumftance, which it may not be impertinent to relate. The compiler of the Cotton ca-talogue (printed at Oxford in 1696), or fome perfon whom he employed, had contented himfelf with defcribing the inestimable vo-lume (Galba E. IX.) which contains fome of the moft precious relics of ancient Eng-lifh poetry in thefe words: "Chaucer. Ex-emplar emendate fcriptum." The manufcript,

---

* Of this monarch, who gave to Chaucer an office in the customs, upon condition that he wrote his accounts with his own hand, it has already been obferved, that, "though adorned with many royal and heroic virtues," he "had not the gift of discerning and patronizing a great poet." Tyrwhitts Chaucer, Appendix to the preface, p. xxviii.

it muft be confefsed, is very *fairly*, and alfo
pretty *correctly* written, (if either be the meaning of *emenaate*,) but owes not the fmalleft
obligation to the great poet whofe genuine
works might, naturally enough, have been
expected to occupy the whole. The indo-
lence of our catalogue-maker being equal to
his ignorance, readyly converted the name of
RICHARD CHAWFER, fcrawled, perhaps by
fome former proprietor of the volume, on a
fpare leaf, into that of GEOFFREY CHAUCER,
the fuppofed author of its contents. To this
fortunate blunder, however, (if a blunder
there was to be,) we are indebted for our acquaintance with the name and writings of
LAURENCE MINOT, whom one of a different
nature might have configned to perpetual
oblivion. The late ingenious and industrious
·mister Tyrwhitt, in preparing materials for
his admirable edition of *The Canterbury tales*,
·confulted the manufcript for the purpofe of

collating an *accurate* copy of his favourite author. His disappointment, which may be eafyly imagined, would be very fpeedyly converted into the moft agreeable furprife, on finding himfelf thus unexpectedly intro-duced to the acquaintance of a new poet, anterior, perhaps, to that favourite in point of time, and certainly not his inferior with refpect to language. In confequence of this happy discovery, the name of LAURENCE MI-NOT (which he himfelf has luckyly taken care to preferve) was firft uſhered into the modern world by a note to the learned " Esſay on the language and verſification of Chaucer."

A copy of thefe poems having been com-municated to mister Warton of Oxford, fome extracts from them appeared, with fuf-ficient aukwardnefs indeed, in the third vo-lume of *The history of Englifh poetry*, pub-liſhed in 1781. Thofe extracts, however, are by no means undistinguifhed by the general inaccuracy which pervades that interefting and important work. Its author, confident in great and fplendid abilities, would feem to have disdained the too fervile tafk of cultivating the acquaintance of ancient dialect or phrafeology, and to have contented himfelf with publifhing, and occafionally attempting to explain, what, it muft be evident, he did not himfelf underftand. That an Englifh writer of the firft eminence fhould never have heard of the name of BALIOL muft excite furprife: and yet this appears to have been the cafe of our poetical historian, who, in his, certainly bold, but not lefs erroneous, attempts to elucidate one of the following poems, makes " Edward THE BALIOLFE" to mean " Edward THE WARLIKE," that is, " Edward THE THIRD," who " is introduced," he fays, " by Minot, as refifting the Scottifh invafion in 1347 [1346] at Nevil's crofs near

Durham;"* though every child might be expected to know that this monarch was, upon
that occasion, at the siege of Calais; and, in
fact, he is, in the very poem alluded to, exprefsly ftated to be " out of the londe." With
refpect to the age of the manufcript, which
the fame gentleman attributes to the reign
of Henry VI. he was probably misled by the
perfon who transmited the poems, as it may
very fairly be refered to that of Richard II.
though fome pieces, it is true, are inferted by
a later hand, and of a more modern date.

* *The* is well known to be the northern corruption of
de: hence *the* Bruce, *the* Baliol, of the Scotifh poets. See
Barbours *Life of Bruce,* pasfim. Thus, alfo, *Philippe* de
Valois is here called *"Philip* the *Valas."* The name of *Baliol*
was frequently written *Bailolf* or *Bailliof* in the age of our
poet. In Moreses *Nomina nobilium equitumque fub E. I.*
1749, we find " fir Thomas de *Bailolf;*" and in a lift of
Durham knights, in the time of Henry III. preferved in an
ancient MS. in the auditors-office, Durham, (called *The
Boldon-buke,* from its containing a copy of that record,) " fir
John de *Bailliof,* fir Hugh de *Bailliof,* fir Euftace de *Bail-
lof."* Blind Harry, the Scotifh Homer, calls John *de Baliol,* " Jhon *the Balzcune."*

That thefe poems were written, or at leaft
completed, in the beginning of the year
1352 (according to the prefent ftile), is not
a mere circumftance of probability, but may '
be clearly demonftrated by internal evidence
and matter of fact. The lateft event they com-
memorate is the capture of Guifnes-castle,
which happened, according to Avesbury, on
faint Vincents day, the 22d of January,
1351-2; and it is manifeft that the conclud-
ing poem, of which that capture is the fub-
ject, was written in "winter", (February, moft
likely,) while the fact was recent, and the cap-
tors were in posfesfion of the place, which,
we learn from Stow, they did not long occupy *. The fact, indeed, might have been

* Stows account, whencefoever he had it, is not every
where very clear. If Avesbury be right, and the ambasfadors
from the earl of Guifnes did not arrive in London before
the day of St. Maurice the abbot, which is the 15th of January, John de Doncaster muft have kept posfesfion till the
following year (1352-3); which is highly improbable.

infered from other circumflances: that the
duke of Lancaster, who is familiarly mentioned by that title, was only fo created the
6th of March 1350-1; and that fome great
events quickly fucceeded the year 1352,
which, as our author has not celebrated nor
alluded to them, it may be prefumed he did
not live to witnefs. Minot, of courfe, is to
be regarded as a poet anterior not only to
Chaucer, who, in 1352, was but 24 years of
age, and had not, fo far as we know, given
any proofs of a poetical imagination, but
alfo to Gower, who, though he furvived that
writer, was probably his fenior by fome years.
He cannot, at the fame time, be confidered
as the firft of Englifh poets, fince, not to
mention the hermit of Hampole, the pro-
lixity of whofe compofitions is compenfated
more by their piety than by their fpirit, he
is clearly posterior to Robert Mannyng (or
of Brunne); whofe namefake of Glouces-

ter is, in fact, the Ennius of this numerous family.*

It seems pretty clear, from our authors dialect and orthography, that he was a native of one of the northern counties, in some monastery whereof the manuscript which contains his poems, along with many others in the same dialect, is conjectured to have been written; and to which, at the same time, it is not improbable that he himself should have belonged. Chance, however, may one day bring us somewhat better acquainted with his history.

* How long Mannyng was employed upon his translation of Langetoft does not appear; but that he had not finished it in 1337 is clear from a pasſage in p. 243 of the printed copy: and, indeed, he, elsewhere, expreſsly tells us,

"Idus that is of May left i to write this ryme,
B letter & Friday bi ix. that zere zede prime."

(p. 341.)

The dominical letter, as Hearne obſerves, ſhould be D: ſo that the poet finiſhed his work, upon which he had probably been engaged for ſome years, on Friday the 15th of May, 1339.

The creative imagination and poetical fancy which distinguish Chaucer, who, considering the general barbarism of his age and country, may be regarded as a prodigy, admit, it muft be acknowledged, of no competition; yet, if the truth may be uttered without offence to the eftablished reputation of that preeminent genius, one may venture to asfert that, in point of eafe, harmony, and variety of verfification, as well as general perfpicuity of ftile, Laurence Minot is, perhaps, equal, if not fuperior, to any English poet before the fixteenth, or even, with very few exceptions, before the feventeenth, century. There are, in fact, but two other poets who are any way remarkable for a particular facility of rimeing and happy choice of words: Robert of Brunne, already mentioned, who wrote before 1340, and Thomas Tusfer, who wrote about 1560.

As to what concerns the prefent publica-
tion, it may be fufficient to fay, that the
poems are printed, with fcrupulous fidelity,
from the only manufcript copy of them
known to exift, of which even the evident
corruptions, though unnoticed in the text
or margin, are not corrected without being
elfewhere pointed out to the reader, in order that he may decide for himfelf upon the
necesfity or propriety of the correction. All
abbreviations, indeed, have been entirely dis-
carded; as hath likewife the character *y*; the
improper reprefentative, though peculiar, perhaps, at that period, to the northern fcribes,
of the Saxon þ. The letter *z*, however, is
retained; a retention which can require no
apology, after the refpectable examples of a
Ruddiman and a Percy; notwithftanding they
may have been ranked, among " ignorant editors," for the prefervation of " this ftupid

blunder."* Its power, at the fame time, is, in thefe poems, everywhere that of the modern *y* confonant; though, on many occafions, it is the fubftitute of *gh*.

It may be requifite to apprife the reader, that our author, like Chaucer, and, perhaps, other poets of the fame age, makes occafional ufe of the *e* feminine, which renders it necesfary, in pronunciation, to divide, in fome cafes, what, in others, is a fingle fyllable: a liberty upon which the metre and harmony of his lines will now and then be found esfentially to depend. Thus, for inftance, in page 1, line 8, the word "dedes" is to be pronounced, as a disfyllable, "dedés"; though, in the very next line but one, it is equally requifite to be pronounced as a monofyllable.

* See *Ancient Scotifh poems*, 1786, p. 520. The asfertion made in the fame page, that the letter *z*, "in the old editions," is "carefully distinguifhed from the" *y* confonant, in the manner there defcribed, feems to be hazarded without the flighteft authority or foundation.

In the fame predicament are " Scottés" (p. 3;
l. 5.) and " Scottes" (p. 4. l. 4.) and " bowés"
(p. 20. l. 10.) and " bowes" (p. 23. l. 4.) The
ufe of the acute accent, which has been introduced in a few inftances of proper names,
may, perhaps, be thought no lefs proper in
the cafe fpoken of; but, befide that there is
only a fingle manufcript, the writer of which,
not having received the terrible injunction
layed upon *Adam fcrivinere* *, was posfibly un-
aware of the poets intention, one muft not
forget the fentiment of a moft ingenious and
accurate perfon upon this fubjeét: that " a
reader, who cannot perform fuch operations
for himself, had better not trouble his head
about the verfification of ' an ancient author'." *   It may, therefor, be deemed fufficient to add, in the words of the fame ex-
cellent critic, that " the true *e* feminine is

* See Urrys *Chaucer*, p. 626.
† *Canterbury tales*, iv. 95.

b

always to be pronounced with an obſcure eva-
neſcent ſound, and is incapable of bearing
any ſtreſs or accent." *

The NOTES which accompany theſe poems
are given chiefly from ſome ancient manu-
ſcript, from the old Engliſh translation of
Froisſart, an almoſt contemporary writer,
and from the chronicles of Fabian, Holin-
ſhed and Stow; but more eſpecially from
that of Froisſart, the extraĉts from which,
though occaſionally prolix, as it is a book
of great rarity, may be excuſed, if not wel-
comed, by moſt readers, on account of their
novelty. The language of this translation,
however obſolete it may now appear, was
doubtleſs eſteemed perfeĉtly elegant at the
court of king Henry the eighth; it being the
work of a very eminent and accompliſhed
nobleman of that period.

* The latter is never implyed by the acute accent '; but
Urry, out of ignorance, adopted the grave accent `, which
always requires it.

As the general information which appeared necesfary to illustrate the two principal
fubjects of Minots poetry, his heros wars with
Scotland and with France, was thought too
long for the notes, it has been thrown into
the form of DISSERTATIONS. This, however, being an after-thought, has occafioned
fome repetitions, which the reader is defired
to pardon.

No word of the leaft difficulty has been intentionally omitted in the GLOSSARY; though
many words, peculiar to our author, are ne-
cesfaryly fubmitted to further investigation;
as it feems no part of an editors duty to fave
his readers the trouble of guefsing at the
meaning of expresfions for which they cannot posfibly be more at a lofs than he is
himself.

DISSERTATIONS.

I.

ON THE SCOTISH WARS OF KING EDWARD III.

THE male line of the royal family of Scotland having become extinct by the death of
Alexander III. in the year 1285-6, and the
young queen, Margaret of Norway, his grand-
daughter, the only furviving defcendant of
Henry prince of Cumberland, eldeft fon of
David I. dying, an infant, in 1290, feveral
perfons, in different rights, layed claim to
the crown; and the regency of Scotland, either unable or unwilling to decide the conteft, folicited the asfistance of king Edward I.
This monarch, powerful, ambitious and po-
litic, readyly accepted the office of arbitra-
tor; but, previously to a decifion upon the
claims of others, he thought it necesfary to

determine a claim of his own, which was, to be fuperior and lord paramount of the kingdom of Scotland; a claim which the competitors, whether through ignorance, timidity, or prudence, unanimoufly acknowleged; and, in that character, they obliged themfelves, by a folemn inftrument, to fubmit to his award: the regency and baronage of Scotland, at the fame time, not only furrendering the kingdom, but doing homage and fwearing fealty, as to their liege lord, in order to enable him, as he pretended, to carry it the more effectually into execution. This meeting was held, by adjournment, at a fmall village on the north fide of the Tweed, oppofite to the castle of Norham, in the beginning of June 1291, and was further adjourned to the 2d of Auguft in the fame year; when the claims were to be received by commisfioners named for the purpofe, who were to report the refult to Edward. The competitors, accord · ingly, at this adjourned meeting, delivered in their claims, which amounted to thirteen; but, moft of them being very frivolous, they were, by different means, finally reduced to two: thofe of John de Baliol and Robert de

Brus, or Bruce, both powerful barons as well
in England as in Scotland; Baliol being the
grandfon of Margaret, the eldeft daughter of
David earl of Huntingdon, fecond fon of
David I. and Bruce the fon of Ifabel, the
fecond daughter of the fame nobleman. The
fole queſtion, therefor, left to the deciſion
of Edward, was whether the iſfue of an elder
fiſter, more remote in one degree, was to
be prefered to the iſfue of a younger fiſter, nearer in one degree; and his definitive
judgement was, that Baliol fhould have feifin of the kingdom of Scotland, faving the
right of the king of England and his heirs.
Seifin being accordingly delivered, Baliol was
crowned at Scone on the 30th of November 1292, and on the 26th of the following
month did homage to his liege lord at New-
caſtle upon Tyne. This adjudication of the
Englifh monarch, however unfatisfactory in
its confequences, was felf-evidently juft; and,
fuppofing with the learned and ingenious
Ruddiman, the Scots of that period to have
thought otherwife, namely, that the child of
a younger daughter was to be prefered, in an
indiviſible inheritance, to the grandchild of

an elder, they muſt certainly have been very confuſed and inconſequential reaſoners.

In the year 1295, Baliol, who had been repeatedly cited before the Engliſh parliament, on the complaint of his own ſubjeƈts, and ſeems, in ſhort, to have had his patience completely, and, perhaps, intentionally, wearyed out by the domineering inſolence of his lord paramount, entered into an alliance with Philip the fair king of France, and committed ſome petty devastation upon the Engliſh borders. Edward, glad of his vasſals rebellion, immediately took Berwick; and, (Baliol having formally renounced his allegiance,) by his general the earl of Warren, defeated the Scots at Dunbar. The castles of Roxburgh, Edinburgh, and Stirling, ſpeedyly ſurrendered; and, to conclude, Baliol, on the 2d of July 1296, in the moſt humiliating manner that could be deviſed, expreſſed contrition for his offences, and reſigned his crown, kingdom, and people into the hands of his liege lord, who once more received the fealty of his Scotiſh ſubjeƈts, as their immediate and lawful ſovereign.

In the following year (1297) the Scots,

under the command of the illustrious William Wallace, defeated the Englifh in repeated engagements, and drove them out of the country. Edward again invaded it, and again, after a fpirited oppofition, reduced it to fubjection. Baliol, whom he had retained in custody from the time of his refignation, was now fent over to France, and delivered into the hands of the popes nuncio, to be dispofed of at his holinefses pleafure. The younger Bruce, who had been chofen one of the guardians of Scotland, in the name of his fathers rival, and had furrendered himfelf to the Englifh, dying in 1304, was, with Edwards confent, fucceeded in his Scotifh inheritances by his eldeft fon.

Edward feemed now to have attained the fummit of his ambitious views: but the calm was tranfient and delufive. Four months fufficed to overthrow a fystem, which, it has been obferved, " the incesfant labours of fifteen years had establifhed by disfimulation, craft, and violence, with a wafte of treafure, and the effufion of much blood."

On the 10th of February 1305-6, Robert

Bruce, grandfon to the competitor, arrived
in Scotland; and, having appointed an interview with John Comyn, lord of Cumber-
nauld, a nobleman of the firft confequence
in that kingdom, in the church of the mi-
norites at Dumfries, ftabbed him before the
high altar. The immediate caufes of Bruce's
leaving the Englifh court, of his requefting
this conference, and of its violent isfue, are
not known. It is, however, highly probable
that he came down refolved to asfert his pretenfions to the Scotifh crown, and, naturally
anxious to attach to his party the moft powerful baron in his realm, had propofed terms,
the rejection of which gave rife to an altercation, which terminated in his opponents
death. But, whatever was, in fact, the fub-
ject of the converfation, to which no third
perfon appears to have been privy, it is certain that Bruce, though excommunicated as
a facrilegious murderer, did not think it necesfary to publifh his vindication. He was
probably fatisfyed in having got rid of one
whofe friendfhip he found it impracticable
to obtain, and whofe enmity might have

furnished an infuperable barrier to his attempt.*

On the 27th of March 1306, Bruce was folemnly crowned at Scone; and, on the 7th of June 1329, dyed in the full and peaceable posfesfion of that fovereignty which he had ftruggled through numerous difficulties, and againft the moft potent enemies, to reftore and eftablifh.

Previously, however, to this event, Edward II. the fon and fuccesfor of Edward I. (who dyed on his expedition againft Scotland, the 7th of July 1307) after a turbulent and disgraceful reign, had, in January 1326-7, been formally depofed from the fovereignty, by the queen and her faction, who had placed his crown on the head of the young prince of Wales, now Edward III. and a treaty of peace between the two kingdoms had been concluded at Northampton in April 1328; of which one article was that Joan, fister to the Englifh monarch, fhould

* The notion, entertained by lord Hailes and others, that Comyn, in right of his mother, Marjory, fister to Baliol, had himfelf fome contingent pretenfions to the crown, feems deftitute of foundation.

be given in marriage to David the only fon
of the king of Scots. This marriage having
accordingly taken place, David II. and his
queen (he being in his 8th year and fhe
about the fame age) were crowned at Scone,
on the 24th of November 1331.

John Baliol, who dyed in France in 1314,
had left an elder fon, Edward, the heir of
his pretenfions; and this youth the king of
England had, in 1330, taken under his protection, and formally permitted to refide
there for a twelvemonth.

Though, by an exprefs article in the treaty
of Northampton, no reftitution was to be
made by either fovereign of inheritances
which had fallen into his hands by the for-
feiture of former proprietors, an exception
was introduced in favour of Thomas lord
Wake, Henry de Beaumont, and Henry de
Percy, who were to be reftored to the eftates
of which the king of Scots, by reafon of the
war between the two nations, had already
taken posfesfion. This article had been ful-
filled with refpect to Percy, and Edward had
repeatedly, though ineffectually, demanded
its performance in favour of Wake and Beau-

mont. Thefe noblemen, therefor, in con-
junction with the other disinherited barous,
having prevailed upon young Baliol, who
arrived very opportunely for their purpofe,
to head the enterprife, determined to invade
Scotland. Edward, however, who affected
publicly to oppofe a defign which he pri-
vately countenanced, would not fuffer them to
enter that kingdom by the Englifh marches;
as fuch a meafure would have been in open
violation of the peace of Northampton, of
which he appeared very tenacious. They,
therefor, changed their plan to an invafion by
fea, and, having embarked with their forces
in the Humber, landed at or near Kinghorn,
in the firth of Forth, on the 6th of Auguft
1332. The earl of Fife, who oppofed their
landing with a few hafty levies, being quickly
defeated, Baliol marched to Dunfermline, and
attacking the Scotifh army under the command of Donald earl of Mar, the new regent, obtained a victory, which to the Englifh was as eafy and honorable, as to the
Scots it is, even by their own historians, al-
lowed to have been bloody and disgraceful.
The regent, whofe ignorance appears to have

been the chief caufe of this national disaster, with many other noblemen, perifhed in the conflict. Baliol entered Perth on the following day, and, a blockade formed by the earl of March being abandoned, within three weeks after his landing perceived himfelf in the peaceable posfesfion of a kingdom, and was formally crowned at Scone on the 24th of September. The king of England now thought it prudent, " for the fafety of the realm," to draw near the Scotifh frontiers; and, while he remained at York, received, from the grateful Baliol, an inftrument, executed at Roxburgh-castle, whereby he acknowleged Edward for his liege lord, and covenanted to put him in posfcsfion of the town of Berwick, and of other territory on the Scotifh marches: offering, moreover, to marry the young queen, to increafe her jointure, and to provide for the dethroned monarch as his faid liege lord fhould advife; and engaging to ferve in all his wars, with two hundred men at arms, for a year together, at his own expence. Edward, in return, was to guarantee the posfesfion of Scotland to this mufhroom monarch. In the mean time the friends of the young king were not idle: for, on the 16th of December following, while Baliol was indulgeing in the fweets of fovereignty at Annan, he was fuddenly attacked by the earl of Murray and others, at the head of a party of horfe, and efcaped with great difficulty into England; his brother, and feveral other perfons of diftinction, being flain in his defence. Here he renewed his engagements to Edward; and, by the asfiftance he received, was enabled to return into Scotland, and quarter himfelf in the neighbourhood of Roxburgh. The Scots, upon Baliols flight, having made fome inroads upon the borders, the Englifh monarch now formally proclaimed that they had violated the peace of Northampton; and, being refolved, he faid, to chaftife their outrages, and to feek redrefs for the injuries which he pretended they had done him, ordered an army to asfemble at Newcastle upon Tyne: defiring, at the fame time, that public prayers might be offered for his fuccefs: a piece of fuperftition or hypocrify which Christian fovereigns take particular care never to neglect when they are engaged in the profecu-

tion of an unjuſt war. He layed ſiege to Berwick, before which Baliol, who had made
him a preſent of it, had already arrived, with
his forces, in the beginning of May 1333;
and, the regent attempting to relieve the
town, a general engagement enſued, at Ha-
lidon-hill, in which the Scots were diſcom-
fited with prodigious ſlaughter; whereupon
the town and fortreſs of Berwick were immediately ſurrendered. The young king and
queen, who had hitherto reſided at Dunbar-
ton caſtle, were now conveyed into France;
and Baliol again held parliaments, in one of
which the treaty of Roxburgh was ratifyed,
and the town, caſtle, and territory of Berwick annexed for ever to the Engliſh crown.
He, ſhortly after, ſurrendered the foreſts of
Jedburgh, Selkirk, and Ettrick, the counties
of Roxburgh, Peebles, Dumfries and Edinburgh, and the conſtabularies of Linlithgow
and Haddington; and, on the 18th of June
1334, did homage, and ſwore fealty, to his
liege lord, for the kingdom of Scotland, at
the town of Newcastle upon Tyne. The par-
tiſans of David, however, ſoon exerted themſelves in ſuch a manner as to oblige Baliol to

implore, in perfon, the protection of his feu-
dal fovereign, who, in December 1334, invaded the country; an invafion which was
repeated in the following year. There would
feem to have been a conteft between this
mock-monarch and his liege lord which of
them could moft effectually wafte and deftroy
a kingdom, which neither had any longer a
hope to enjoy peaceably.* The war was carryed on with various fuccefs till May 1341,
when (Baliol having previously withdrawn
into England) David and his queen arrived
from France. The Scots now began to reta-
liate on the Englifh frontiers; and, in 1346,
while Edward was profecuting his wars in
France, David, at the inftigation, it is faid,
of king Philip, whom the Englifh monarch
had already charged with aiding the Scots
contrary to the conditions of a fubfifting truce,
asfembled a formidable army, and, penetrat-
ing into the bifhopric of Durham, pitched

---

* Another pretender, according to Wyntown, ftarted up
in the perfon of John of Eltham, earl of Cornwall, only
brother to the king of England, whom, in the heat of their
altercation upon the fubjeft, he flew with his own hand.
(See B. VIII. c. xxx.)

his camp in the neighbourhood of that city, on the 16th of October. The archbifhop of York (William de la Zouche), Henry de Percy, and Ralph de Nevill, under a commisfion from the regency, headed the Englifh army; and, in an engagement which enfued, called *The battle of Nevils-crofs*, the Scots were routed with great flaughter, and their king, after a gallant refistance, taken prifoner: nor, though occafionally permitted to vifit his dominions, was he finally releafed till the 3d of October 1357, after a captivity of eleven years.

Baliol, who had ferved in the Englifh army at the battle of Durham, and, from king of Scotland, condefcended to become governor of Berwick, feeming now completely fick of fovereignty, made an abfolute furrender to Edward, in confideration of 5000 marks and an annuity of 2000£. as well of his private eftates in Scotland as of his nominal kingdom, delivering feifin of the former by a clod of earth, and of the latter by the royal diadem, and inferting in the inftrument of furrender a claufe of warranty for himfelf and his heirs againft all mortals for ever.

This farcical fcene pafsed at Roxburgh-castle, while Edward, it feems, lay at Bamburgh in Northumberland; and the phantom of departed royalty, who appears, throughout the procefs of this political drama, the tool of the more crafty and ambitious Edward, retired into England, where he continued in obfcurity till the time of his death, which happened in 1363.

Edward, now become the immediate and abfolute fovereign of Scotland, displayed his affection for his new fubjeдs by a frefh inroad and more extenfive devastation; being "refolved," he faid, "inviolably to maintain the ancient laws and the ufages of that kingdom." The Englifh, however, were foon driven out of the country, and the liege lord and asfignee of Baliol finally "exprefsed his willingnefs to enter into a treaty with the Scots, not only for the ranfom of their king, and for a cesfation of hostilities, but alfo for a perpetual peace."*

* See the *Annals of Scotland*, by fir David Dalrymple (lord Hailes). Edin. 1776-9, 2 vols. 4to.

II.

ON the death of Charles the fair, king of
France, the laſt of the three ſons and ſucces-
ſors of Philip the fair, in 1328, (his wife,
Joan d'Evreux, being left pregnant,) the office of regent was claimed by Edward III.
king of England, then a youth of 15, in
right of his mother Iſabel, only ſister of the
deceaſed monarch; his claim being oppoſed
by that of Philip, ſon of Charles, of Valois,
younger brother of Philip the fair. This con-
teſt (which involved, in faɛt, the right of ſuc-
cesſion to the crown itſelf, in caſe the child
of which Joan was then pregnant ſhould, as
it did, happen to be a daughter), was, by the
French peerage, decided in favour of the latter, who, in virtue of that deciſion, on the
delivery of the queen-dowager, ſucceeded to
the vacant throne. In any other country
than France the claim of Edward muſt un-

questionably have been prefered to that of
Philip; but by an ancient and eftablifhed
custom of that kingdom (ufually called the
Salic law) females were incapable of inhe-
riting the crown; and, confequently, Ifabel,
having no right in herfelf, could not posfibly, as was contended, transmit any to her
fon. This confequence, however, was denyed
by Edward, who infifted, that, although females were perfonally excluded, fuch inca-
pacity did not reach their male defcendants;
and that he, as the neareft male in blood,
ought to be prefered to Philip, who was
very far removed. But the argument, if
well-founded, clearly proved too much to
be of any fervice to the Englifh monarch,
fince the male isfue of the daughters of former kings muft inevitably have been prefered
to him. Thofe writers who have argued
againft the existence or force of the law itfelf
have fallen into a fimilar dilemma; fince, it
is evident, allowing the defcent of the crown
to females, that the pretenfions of Edward,
however preferable to thofe of Philip, muft
have been poftponed to the right even of
Blanch the new-born daughter of the late

king. The validity, therefor, of the Salic law was necefsaryly admitted by both parties; the only disagreement between them arifing from its conftruction. The fallacy of Edwards claim is manifefted by his own arguments: fince, in the firft place, if the right of the mother were nothing, fhe, whether living (as fhe then was) or dead, could transmit none to the fon; and, fecondly, if fhe had a right capable of transmisfion, the male isfue of Joan daughter of Lewis Hutin, of Joan daughter of Philip the long, and of Blanch daughter of Charles the fair, were clearly to be prefered to the male isfue of Ifabel the fister of thofe monarchs. It is, therefor, impossible to conceive a claim more frivolous and worfe fupported than that of Edward to the crown of France. However, as the reafoning of kings is faid to confift in force, to that fpecies of logic the disappointed monarch, as foon as he found it convenient, was determined to refort.

Soon after the coronation of Philip of Valois (*A. C.* 1329), Edward, who held the duchy of Aquitain and county of Ponthieu as a vasfal to the crown of France, was fummoned to do his fealty for thofe provinces. This threw him into a great dilemma; for, if he fhould refufe the required homage, he muſt inevitably forfeit his territories, which he did not at that period think himfelf ſtrong enough to defend; and, if he performed it, he would, by acknowlegeing the fuperiority of Philip, appear to renounce his pretenfions to the kingdom itfelf. Out of this difficulty he was extricated by a falvo worthy of his claim: he protefted, in a council of his peers, that whatever he was about to perform or promife in France would be done againſt his will, and to the end only that he might pre-ferve his provinces in that kingdom; of which, after a trifling objection as to the nature of the homage, he received the accuſtomed in-veſtiture.

In the year 1336, after the conclufion of the Scotifh wars, Edward began to think it time that he fhould convince Philip of his fuperior right to the throne of France by force of arms. To this projeＣt he is generally thought to have been determined by the in-flammatory eloquence of Robert earl of Ar-tois, a French refugee, who, to gratify a perfonal pique againft his fovereign, fcrupled not to endeavour the deftruction of his coun- try; but there can be little doubt that Ed- ward was fufficiently inclined to the mea- fures he adopted without fuch diabolical in- ftigation. With this view he formed alliances with many illuftrious potentates on the con- tinent; amongft whom were the duke of Brabant, the marquis of Juliers, the earls of Gelderland and Hainault, the archbifhop of Cologne, and, finally, the emperor, Lewis of Bavaria, who created him vicar of the em- pire throughout France, which gave him a colourable authority over his German confe- derates. James Arteville, likewife, a brewer of Ghent, who had acquired the management of the turbulent Flemings, brought that pow- erful nation into the league; and, in order to avoid the penalty or reproach of taking up arms againft *the king of France*, with whom they had lately concluded a treaty of peace, perfuaded Edward to asfume that title: but which, it is faid, the monarch, as if con- fcious of the flagrant injuftice of the ufurpa- tion, was not prevailed on to do without he- fitation and difficulty. He now, however, fent

the duke of Brabant and marquis of Juliers in
formal embasfy to Philip to demand a refignation of the crown; he publifhed manifestos,
and wrote letters to the pope: the former, of
courfe, Philip declined, and the latter he re-
futed or replyed to. The two firft campaigns,
if Edwards invafions of France may be fo
called, pafsed without any action of importance; and a truce, on the intercesfion of the
countefs of Hainault, the mother-in-law of
Edward and fister of Philip, was agreed to
by thefe rival monarchs. In the mean time,
Edwards German allies, disappointed probably in their too fanguine expectations of
Englifh gold and French plunder, graduallŷ
fell off; and even the emperor, at the inftance of Philip, revoked the title of impe-
rial vicar.

On the expiration of the truce, the war
was renewed with increased vigour, and the
fuccefses of the campaign were crowned by
the bloody victory of Cresfy, and the long-
expected furrender of Calais. A new truce
was now concluded on, through the media-
tion of the popes legates, during which Philip of Valois dyed, and was fucceeded by his

fon John, who, on a renewal of the war, was made prifoner at the battle of Poictiers in 1356. This event was followed by another truce for two years; and Edwards terms of pacification, though accepted by his royal captive, being rejected, as dishonorable and injurious, by the dauphin and ftates of France, he, in 1359, prepared for a new invafion of that unfortunate kingdom, which accordingly took place; but, becoming fenfible that the fuccefs of his arms anfwered no other purpofe than to depopulate one country and impoverifh the other, he was induced to liften to more reafonable propofals, and a peace was, at length, concluded, on the 8th of May 1360, of which the principal conditions were, that king John fhould be fet at liberty, on payment of three million crowns of gold; that Edward fhould for ever renounce all claim to the crown of France, as well as to the provinces of Normandy, Maine, Touraine and Anjou, posfefsed by his ancestors; in lieu whereof he was to receive certain other districts, together with the towns of Calais, Guifnes and Montreuil, to be held, along with Guienne, in abfolute fovcreignty: but John, finding

infuperable difficulties to occur in fulfilling
the conditions of the peace on his part, gave
a fingular proof of monarchical good faith,
by returning to his former lodgings in the
Savoy, where he dyed on the 8th of April
1364.

The power and posfefsions of the Englifh
every day yielding to the prudence of the new
king, Charles V. and the conduct of his brave
conftable, Du Guefclin, Edward thought fit
to refume the empty title of king of France;*
but, after fending repeated though ineffec-
tual levies into that kingdom, was at length
obliged to conclude a truce with the enemy,
"after almoft all his ancient posfefsions,"
fays Hume, "had been ravifhed from him,

* This title has fince continued a part of the royal ftile,
and, by an act of parliament, made in the 35th year of
Henry VIII. was "united and annexed for ever to the im-
perial crown of his highnefs realm of England:" as if it
confifted with the peculiar morality of kings and nations to
perpetuate, with ostentatious and infulting formality, an inftance of ufurpation and injustice which had been the means
of converting an unnatural hatred into a national virtue, of
wafting millions of treafure, and of fpilling oceans of blood.
It has now, indeed, loft its baneful influence, and is become
perfectly infignificant and contemptible.

except Bourdeaux and Bayonne, and all his new conquefts, except Calais." Having furvived his eldeft fon, the black prince, about a year, he expired on the 21ft of June 1377, in the 65th year of his age and the 51ft of his reign.*

* See *Schoepflini commentationes historicæ & criticæ. Bafiliæ*, 1741. 4to. *caput V.* and Humes *History of England*, volume II.

POEMS.

I.

LITHES, AND I SALL TELL ZOW TYLL
THE BATAILE OF HALIDON-HYLL.

TREW king, that fittes in trone,
   Unto the i tell my tale,
And unto the i bid a bone,
   For thou ert bute of all my bale:
Als thou made midelerd and the mone,
   And beftes and fowles grete and fmale,
Unto me fend thi focore fone,
   And drefce my dedes in this dale.

B

In this dale i droupe and dare,
　　For dern dedes that done me dere;
Of Ingland had my hert grete care,
　　When Edward founded firſt to were:
The Franche-men war frek to fare
　　Ogaines him, with ſcheld and ſpere;
Thai turned ogayn, with ſides ſare,
　　And al thaire pomp noght worth a pere.

A pere of priſe es more ſum tyde
　　Than al the boſte of Normondye:
Thai ſent thaire ſchippes on ilka ſide,
　　With fleſch and wine, and whete and rye;
With hert and hand (es noght at hide)
　　For to help Scotland gan thai hye:
Thai fled, and durſt no dede habide,
　　And all thaire fare noght wurth a flye.

For all thaire fare, thai durſt noght fight,
　　For dedes dint had thai ſlike dout;
Of Scotland had thai never fight,
　　Ay whils thai war of wordes ſtout:
Thai wald have mend tham at thaire might,
　　And beſy war thai thareobout.
Now god help Edward in his right!
　　Amen! and all his redy rowt!

His redy rout mot Jhefu fpede,
　And fave tham both by night and day;
That lord of hevyn mot Edward lede,
　And maintene him als he wele may.
The Scottes now all wide will fprede,
　For thai have failed of thaire pray;
Now er thai dareand all for drede,
　That war bifore fo ftout and gay.

Gai thai war, and wele thai thoght
　On the erle Morré and other ma;
Thai faid it fuld ful dere be boght,
　The land that thai war flemid fra.
Philip Valays wordes wroght,
　And faid he fuld thaire enmys fla :
Bot all thaire wordes was for noght,
　Thai mun be met if thai war ma.

Ma manafinges zit have thai maked,
　Mawgre mot thai have to mede !
And many nightes als have thai waked
　To dere all Ingland with thaire dede :
Bot, loved be god ! the pride es flaked
　Of tham that war fo ftout on ftede;
And fum of tham es levid all naked,
　Noght fer fro Berwik opon Twede.

A litell fro that forſaid toune,
　Halydon-hill that es the name,
Thare was crakked many a crowne
　Of wild Scottes, and alls of tame ;
Thare was thaire baner born all doune;
　To mak ſlike boſte thai war to blame :
Bot nevertheles ay er thai boune
　To wait Ingland with ſorow and ſchame.

Shame thai have, als I here ſay;
　At Dondé now es done thaire daunce,
And wend thai moſt another way,
　Even thurgh Flandres into France:
On Filip Valas faſt cri thai,
　Thare for to dwell and him avaunce ;
And nothing liſt tham than of play,
　Sen tham es tide this ſary chance.

This ſary chaunce tham es bitid,
　For thai war fals and wonder fell;
For curſed caitefes er thai kid,
　And ful of treſon, ſuth to tell.
Sir Jon the Comyn had thai hid,
　In haly kirk thai did him qwell;
And tharfore many a Skottis brid
　With dole er dight that thai moſt dwell.

Thare dwelled oure king, the futh to faine,
  With his menzè, a litell while;
He gaf gude confort, on that plaine,
  To all his men obout a myle.
All if his men war mekill of maine,
  Ever thai douted tham of gile;
The Scottes gaudes might nothing gain,
  For all thai ftumbilde at that ftile.

Thus in that ftowre thai left thaire live,
  That war bifore fo proud in prefe.
Jhefu, for thi woundes five,
  In Ingland help us to have pefe!

II.

SKOTTES, out of Berwik and of Abirdene,
At the Bannokburn war ze to kene;
Thare flogh ze many fakles, als it was fene,
And now has king Edward wroken it, i wene:
It es wroken i wene, wele wurth the while;
War zit with the Skottes, for thai er ful of gile.

Whare er ze, Skottes of Saint-Johnes-toune?
The bofte of zowre baner es betin all doune;
When ze bofting will bede, fir Edward es boune
For to kindel zow care, and crak zowre crowne:
He has crakked zowre croune, wele worth the while;
Schame bityde the Skottes, for thai er full of gile.

Skottes of Striflin war fteren and ftout,
Of god ne of gude men had thai no dout;
Now have thai the pelers priked obout,
Bot at the laft fir Edward rifild thaire rout:
He has rifild thaire rout, wele wurth the while;
Bot ever er thai under bot gaudes and gile.

Rughfute-riveling, now kindels thi care,
Bere-bag, with thi bofte, thi biging es bare;
Fals wretche and forfworn, whider wiltou fare?
Bufk the unto brig, and abide thare :
Thare, wretche, faltou won, and wery the while;
Thi dwelling in Dondé es done for thi gile.

The Skotte gafe in burghes, and betes the ftretes,
All thife Inglis-men harmes he hetes;
Faft makes he his mone to men that he metes,
Bot fone frendes he findes that his bale betes :
Fune betes his bale, wele wurth the while;
He ufes all threting with gaudes and gile.

Bot many man thretes and fpekes ful ill,
That fum tyme war better to be ftane-ftill;
The Skot in his wordes has wind for to fpill,
For at the laft Edward fall have al his will :
He had his will at Berwik, wele wurth the while.
Skottes broght him the kayes, bot get for thaire gile.

III.

God, that fchope both fe and fand,
Save Edward king of Ingland,
Both body, faul and life,
And grante him joy withowten ftrif;
For mani men to him er wroth,
In Fraunce and in Flandres both:
For he defendes faft his right,
And tharto Jhefu grante him might,
And fo to do, both night and day,
That yt may be to goddes pay.
    Oure king was cumen, trewly to tell,
Into Brabant for to dwell;
The kayfer Lowis of Bavere,
That in that land than had no pere,
He, and als his fons two,
And other princes many mo,
Bisfchoppes and prelates war thare fele,
That had ful mekill werldly wele,
Princes and pople, ald and zong,
Al that fpac with Duche tung,

All thai come with grete honowre,
Sir Edward to fave and focoure,
And proferd him, with all thayre rede,
For to hald the kinges ftede.
The duke of Braband, firft of all,
Swore, for thing that might bifall,
That he fuld, both day and night,
Help fir Edward in his right,
In toun, in feld, in frith and fen;
This fwore the duke and all his men,
And al the lordes that with him lend,
And tharto held thai up thaire hend.
Than king Edward toke his reft,
At Andwerp, whare him liked beft;
And thare he made his moné playne,
That no man fuld fay thareogayne;
His moné, that was gude and lele,
Left in Braband ful mekill dele;
And all that land, untill this day,
Fars the better for that jornay.
When Philip the Valas herd of this,
Tharat he was ful wroth, i wis;
He gert asfemble his barounes,
Princes and lordes of many tounes;
At Parifs toke thai thaire counfaile,
Whilke pointes might tham mofte availe;

And in all wife thai tham bithoght
To ftroy Ingland, and bring to noght.
Schip-men fone war efter fent,
To here the kinges cumandment;
And the galaies-men alfo,
That wift both of wele and wo.
He cumand than that men fuld fare
Till Ingland, and for nothing fpare,
Bot brin and fla both man and wife,
And childe, that none fuld pas with life :
The galay-men held up thaire handes,
And thanked god of thir tithandes.
At Hamton, als i underftand,
Come the gaylayes unto land,
And ful faft thai flogh and brend,
Bot noght fo mekill als fum men wend;
For or thai wened war thai mett
With men that fone thaire laykes lett.
Sum was knokked on the hevyd,
That the body thare bilevid;
Sum lay ftareand on the fternes;
And fum lay knoked out thaire hernes:
Than with tham was none other gle,
Bot ful fain war thai that might fle.
The galay-men, the futh to fay,
Moft nedes turn another way;

Thai foght the ftremis fer and wide,
Jn Flandres and in Seland fyde.
Than faw thai whare Cristofer ftode,
At Armouth, opon the flude;
Than wen thai theder all bidene,
The galayes-men, with hertes kene,
Eight and forty galays and mo,
And with tham als war tarettes two,
And other many of galiotes,
With grete noumber of fmale botes;
Al thai hoved on the flode,
To ftele fir Edward mens gode.
Edward oure king than was noght there,
Bot fone, when it come to his ere,
He fembled all his men full ftill,
And faid to tham what was his will.
Ilk man made him redy then,
So went the king and all his men
Unto thaire fchippes ful haftily,
Als men that war in dede doghty.
Thai fand the galay-men, grete wane,
A hundereth ever ogaynes ane;
The Inglis-men put tham to were,
Ful baldly, with bow and fpere;
Thai flogh thare of the galaies-men,
Ever fexty ogaynes ten;

That fum ligges zit in that mire,
All hevidles withowten hire.
The Inglis-men war armed wele,
Both in yren and in ftele;
Thai faght ful faft, both day and night,
Als lang als tham lafted might;
Bot galay-men war fo many,
That Inglis-men wex all wery:
Help thai foght, bot thar come nane,
Than unto god thai made thaire mane.
Bot, fen the time that god was born,
Ne a hundreth zere biforn,
War never men better in fight
Than Inglifs-men, while thai had myght;
Bot, fone all maistri gan thai mis.
God bring thaire faules untill his blis!
And god asfoyl tham of thaire fin,
For the gude will that thai war in! Amen.
    Liftens now, and leves me,
Who fo lifes thai fall fe
That it mun be ful dere boght,
That thir galay-men have wroght.
Thai hoved ftill opon the flode,
And reved pover men thaire gude;
Thai robbed, and did mekill fchame,
And ay bare Inglis-men the blame.

Now Jhefu fave all Ingland,
And blis it with his haly hand! Amen.

EDWARD, oure cumly king,
In Braband has his woning,
   With mani cumly knight;
And in that land, trewly to tell,
Ordains he ftill for to dwell,
   To time he think to fight.

Now god, that es of mightes mafte,
Grant him grace of the haly gafte,
   His heritage to win;
And Mari moder, of mercy fre,
Save oure king and his menze
   Fro forow, fchame and fyn.

Thus in Braband has he bene,
Whare he bifore was feldom fene,
   For to prove thaire japes;
Now no langer wil he fpare,
Bot unto Fraunce faft will he fare,
   To confort hym with grapes.

Furth he ferd into France,
God fave him fro mischance,
   And all his cumpany !

The nobill duc of Braband
With him went into that land,
  Redy to lif or dy.

Than the riche floure de lice
Wan thare ful litill prife,
  Faft he fled for ferde;
The right aire of that cuntre
Es cumen, with all his knightes fre,
  To fchac him by the berd.

Sir Philip the Valayfe
Wit his men in tho dayes,
  To batale had he thoght;
He bad his men tham purvay,
Withowten lenger delay,
  Bot he ne held it noght.

He broght folk, ful grete wone,
Ay fevyn ogains one,
  That ful wele wapind were;
Bot fone when he herd afcry
That king Edward was nere tharby,
  Than durft he noght cum nere.

In that morning fell a myft,
And when oure Inglifs-men it wift,
  It changed all thaire chere;

Oure king unto god made his bone,
And god fent him gude confort fone,
   The wedeȟ wex ful clere.

Oure king and his men held the felde
Stalworthly, with fpere and fchelde,
   And thoght to win his right,
With lordes, and with knightes kene,
And other doghty men bydene,
   That war ful frek to fight.

When fir Philip of France herd tell
That king Edward in feld walld dwell,
   Than gayned him no gle;
He traifted of no better bote,
Bot both on hors and on fote
   He hafted him to fle.

It femid he was ferd for ftrokes
When he did fell his grete okes
   Obout his pavilyoune;
Abated was than all his pride,
For langer thare durft he noght bide,
   His boft was broght all doune.

The king of Beme had cares colde,
That was ful hardy and bolde,
   A ftede to umftride;

[He and] the king als of Naverne
War faire ferd in the ferne
   Thaire heviddes for to hide.

And leves wele it es no lye,
The felde hat Flemangrye
   That king Edward was in,
With princes that war ftif ande bolde,
And dukes that war doghty tolde,
   In batayle to bigin.

The princes that war riche on raw
Gert nakers ftrike, and trumpes blaw,
   And made mirth at thaire might;
Both alblaft and many a bow
War redy railed opon a row,
   And ful frek for to fight.

Gladly thai gaf mete and drink,
So that thai fuld the better fwink,
   The wight men that thar ware.
Sir Philip of Fraunce fled for dout,
And hied him hame with all his rout:
   Coward, god giff him care!

For thare than had the lely-flowre
Lorn all halely his honowre,
   That fo gat fled for ferd;

Bot oure king Edward come ful ftill,
When that he trowed no harm him till,
  And keped him in the berde.

IV.

Minot with mowth had menid to make
Suth fawes and fad for fum mens fake;
The wordes of fir Edward makes me to wake,
Wald he falve us fone mi forow fuld flake;
War mi forow flaked fune wald I fing:
When god will fir Edward fal us bute bring.
Sir Philip the Valas caft was in care,
And faid fir Hugh Kyret to Flandres fuld fare,
And have Normondes inogh to leve on his lare,
All Flandres to brin, and mak it all bare;
Bot, unkind coward, wo was him thare,
When he failed in the Swin it fowed him fare;
Sare it tham fmerted that ferd out of France,
Thare lered Inglis-men tham a new daunce.
The burjafe of Bruge ne war noght to blame,
I pray Jhefu fave tham fro fin and fro fchame;
For thai war fone at the Slufe all by a name,
Whare many of the Normandes tok mekill grame.

When Bruges and Ipyre hereof herd tell,
Thai fent Edward to wit, that was in Arwell;
Than had he no liking langer to dwell,
He hafted him to the Swin, with fergantes fnell,
To mete with the Normandes that fals war and fell,
That had ment, if thai might, al Flandres to quell.
King Edward unto fail was ful fune dight,
With erles and barons, and many kene knight;
Thai come byfor Blankebergh on faint Jons night,
That was to the Normondes a well fary fight;
Zit trumped thai and daunced, with torches ful bright
In the wilde waniand was thaire hertes light.
Opon the morn efter, if i futh fay,
A mery man, fir Robard out of Morlay,
At half-eb in the Swin foght he the way,
Thare lered men the Normandes at bukler to play;
Helpid tham no prayer that thai might pray,
The wreches es wonnen, thaire wapin es oway.
The erle of Norhamton helpid at that nede,
Als wife man of wordes, and worthli in wede.
Sir Walter the Mawnay, god gif him mede!
Was bold of body in batayle to bede.
The duc of Lankaster was dight for to drive,
With mani mody man that thoght for to thrive;
Wele and ftalworthly ftint he that ftrive,
That few of the Normandes left thai olive;

Fone left thai olive, bot did tham to lepe,
Men may find by the flode a hundred on hepe.
Sir Wiliam of Klinton was eth for to knaw,
Mani ftout bachilere broght he on raw;
It femid with thaire fchoting als it war fnaw,
The boft of the Normandes broght thai ful law;
Thaire boft was abated, and thaire mekil pride,
Fer might thai noght fle, bot thaire bud tham bide.
The gude erle of Glowceter, god mot him glade!
Broght many bold men with bowes ful brade;
To biker with the Normandes baldely thai bade,
And in middes the flode did tham to wade;
To wade war tho wretches caften in the brim,
The kaitefs come out of France at lere tham to fwim.
I prays John Badding als one of the beft;
Faire come he fayland out of the futh-weft,
To prove of tha Normandes was he ful preft,
Till he had foghten his fill he had never reft.
John of Aile of the Sluys, with fcheltron full fchene,
Was comen into Cagent, cantly and kene;
Bot fone was his trumping turned to tene,
Of him had fir Edward his will, als i wene.
The fchipmen of Ingland failed ful fwith,
That none of the Normandes fro tham might fkrith:
Whofo kouth wele his craft thare might it kith;
Of al the gude that thai gat gaf thai no tithe.

Two hundreth and mo fchippes in the fandes
Had oure Inglis-men won with thaire handes;
The Kogges of Ingland was broght out of bandes,
And alfo the Cristofir, that in the ftreme ftandes;
In that ftound thai ftode with ftremers ful ftil,
Till thai wift ful wele fir Edwardes will.
Sir Edward, oure gude king, wurthi in wall,
Faght wele on that flude, faire mot him fall!
Als it es custom of king to confort tham all,
So thanked he gudely the grete and the fmall;
He thanked tham gudely, god gif him mede!
Thus come our king in the Swin till that gude dede.
This was the bataile that fell in the Swin,
Where many Normandes made mekill din;
Wele war thai armed up to the chin,
Bot god and fir Edward gert thaire bofte blin;
Thus blinned thaire bofte, als we wele ken:
God asfoyle thaire fawls! fais all Amen.

V.

Towrenay zow has tight
  To timber, trey and tene;
A bore with brems bright,
  Es broght opon zowre grene;
That es a femely fight,
  With fchilterouns faire and fchene:
Thi domes-day es dight,
  Bot thou be war, I wene.

When all yowre wele es went
  Zowre wo wakkins ful wide,
To fighing er ze fent
  With forow on ilka fyde;
Ful rewfull es zowre rent,
  All redles may ze ride;
The harmes that ze have hent
  Now may ze hele and hide.

Hides and helis als hende,
  For ze er caft in care,
Ful few find ze zowre frende,

For all zowre frankis fare.
Sir Philip fall zow fchende,
   Whi leve ze at his lare?
No bowes now thar zow bende,
   Of blis ze er all bare.

All bare er ze of blis,
   No boft may be zowre bote,
All mirthes mun ze mis,
   Oure men fall with zow mote,
Who fall zow clip and kys,
   And fall zowre folk to fote;
A were es wroght, i wis,
   Zowre walles with to wrote.

Wrote thai fal zowre dene,
   Of dintes ze may zow dowt;
Zowre biginges fall men brene,
   And breke zowre walles obout.
Ful redles may ze ren,
   With all zowre rewful rout;
With care men fall zow ken
   Edward zowre lord to lout.

To lout zowre lord in land
   With lift men fall zow lere;
Zowre harmes cumes at hand,

Als ze fall haftly here.
Now frendfchip fuld ze fande
Of fir Philip zowre fere,
To bring zow out of band,
Or ze be broght on bere.

On bere when ze er broght,
Than cumes Philip to late;
He hetes, and haldes zow noght,
With hert ze may him hate.
A bare now has him foght
Till Turnay the right gate,
That es ful wele bithoght
To ftop Philip the ftrate,
Ful ftill:
Philip was fain he moght
Graunt fir Edward his will.

If ze will trow my tale,
A duke tuke leve that tide,
A Braban brwed that bale,
He bad no langer bide;
Giftes grete and fmale
War fent him on his fide;
Gold gert all that gale,
And made him rapely ride,
Till dede:

In hert he was unhale,
   He come thare mofte for mede.

King Edward, frely fode,
   In Fraúnce he will noght blin
To mak his famen wode,
   That er wonand tharein.
God, that reft òn rode,
   For fake of Adams fyn,
Strenkith him main and mode,
   His reght in France to win,
            And have!
God grante him graces gode,
   And fro all fins us fave! Amen.

VI.

HOW EDWARD AT HOGGES UNTO LAND WAN
AND RADE THURGH FRANCE OR EVER HE BLAN

MEN may rede in romance right
Of a grete clerk that Merlin hight;
Ful many bokes er of him wreten,
Als thir clerkes wele may witten;
And zit, in many prevé nokes,
May men find of Merlin bokes.
Merlin faid thus, with his mowth,
Out of the north into the fowth
Suld cum a bare over the fe,
That fuld mak many man to fle;
And in the fe, he faid ful right,
Suld he fchew ful mekill might;
And in France he fuld bigin
To mak tham wrath that er tharein;
Untill the fe his taile reche fale
All folk of France to mekill bale.
Thus have i mater for to make,
For a nobill prince fake:
Help me god, my wit es thin!
Now LAURENCE MINOT will bigin.

A BORE es broght on bankes bare,
　With ful batail bifor his breſt,
For John of France will he noght ſpare,
　In Normondy to tak his reſt,
With princes that er proper and preſt :
　Alweldand god, of mightes maſte,
He be his beld, for he mai beſt,
　Fader and ſun and haly gaſte!

Haly gaſte, thou gif him grace,
　That he in gude time may bigin,
And ſend to him both might and ſpace,
　His heritage wele for to win ;
And ſone asſoyl him of his ſin,
　Hende god, that heried hell !
For France now es he entred in,
　And thare he dightes him for to dwell.

He dwelled thare, the ſuth to tell,
　Opon the coſte of Normondy ;
At Hogges fand he famen fell,
　That war all ful of felony :
To him thai makked grete maistri,
　And proved to ger the bare abyde ;
Thurgh might of god and mild Mari,
　The bare abated all thaire pride.

Mekill pride was thare in prefe,
　　Both on pencell and on plate,
When the bare rade, withouten refe,
　　Unto Cane the graytheft gate;
Thare fand he folk bifor the zate
　　Thretty-thowfand ftif on ftede:
Sir John of France come al to late,
　　The bare has gert thaire fides blede.

He gert blede if thai war bolde,
　　For thare was flayne and wounded fore
Thretty-thowfand, trewly tolde,
　　Of pitaile was thare mekill more;
Knightes war thar wele two fcore,
　　That war new dubbed to that dance,
Helm and hevyd thai have forlore:
　　Than misliked John of France.

More misliking was thare then,
　　For fals trefon alway thai wroght;
Bot, fro thai met with Inglis-men,
　　All thaire bargan dere thai boght.
Inglis-men with fite tham foght,
　　And haftily quit tham thaire hire;
And, at the laft, forgat thai noght,
　　The toun of Cane thai fett on fire.

That fire ful many folk gan fere,
  When thai fe brandes o ferrum flye;
This have thai wonen of the were,
  The fals folk of Normundy.
I fai zow lely how thai lye,
  Dongen doun all in a daunce;
Thaire frendes may ful faire forthi
  Pleyn tham untill John of France.

Franche-men put tham to pine,
  At Cresfy, when thai brak the brig;
That faw Edward with both his ine,
  Than likid him no langer to lig.
Ilk Inglis-man on others rig,
  Over that water er thai went;
To batail er thai baldly big,
  With brade ax, and with bowes bent.

With bent bowes thai war ful bolde,
  For to fell of the Frankifch-men;
Thai gert tham lig with cares colde,
  Ful fari was fir Philip then.
He faw the toun o ferrum bren,
  And folk for ferd war faft fleand;
The teres he lete ful rathly ren
  Out of his eghen, i underftand..

Than come Philip, ful redy dight,
   Toward the toun, with all his rowt,
With him come mani a kumly knight,
   And all umſet the bare obout.
The bare made tham ful law to lout,
   And delt tham knokkes to thaire mede;
He gert tham ſtumbill that war ſtout,
   Thare helpid nowther ſtaf ne ſtede.

Stedes ſtrong bilevid ſtill
   Biſide Creſfy opon the grene;
Sir Philip wanted all his will,
   That was wele on his ſembland ſene.
With ſpere and ſchelde and helmis ſchene,
   The bare than durſt thai noght habide:
The king of Beme was cant and kene,
   Bot thare he left both play and pride.

Pride in preſe ne prais i noght,
   Omang thir princes prowd in pall;
Princes ſuld be wele bithoght,
   When kinges ſuld tham tyll counſail call
If he be rightwis king, thai ſall
   Maintene him both night and day,
Or els to lat his frendſchip fall
   On faire manere, and fare oway.

Oway es all thi wele, i wis,
  Frauche-man, with all thi fare;
Of murning may thou never mys,
  For thou ert cumberd all in care:
With fpeche ne moght thou never fpare
  To fpeke of Inglifs-men defpite;
Now have thai made thi biging bare,
  Of all thi catell ertou quite.

Quite ertou, that wele we knaw,
  Of catell, and of drewris dere,
Tharfore lies thi hert ful law,
  That are was blith als brid on brere.
Inglis-men fall zit to-zere
  Knok thi palet or thou pas,
And mak the polled like a frere;
  And zit es Ingland als it was.

Was thou noght, Franceis, with thi wapin,
  Bitwixen Cresfy and Abvyle,
Whare thi felaws lien and gapin,
  For all thaire treget and thaire gile?
Bisfchoppes war thare in that while,
  That fongen all withouten ftole:
Philip the Valas was a file,
  He fled, and durft noght tak his dole.

Men delid thare ful mani a dint
  Omang the gentill Geneuayfe;
Ful many man thaire lives tint,
  For luf of Philip the Valays.
Unkind he was and uncurtayfe,
  I prais nothing his purviance;
The beft of France and of Artayfe
  War al to-dongyn in that daunce.

That daunce with trefon was bygun,
  To trais the bare with fum fals gyn:
The Franche-men faid, All es wun,
  Now es it tyme that we bigin;
For here es welth inogh to win,
  To make us riche for evermore:
Bot, thurgh thaire armure thik and thin,
  Slaine thai war, and wounded fore.

Sore than fighed fir Philip,
  Now wift he never what him was beft;
For he es caft doun with a trip,
  In John of France es all his treft;
For he was his frend faithfuleft,
  In him was full his affiance:
Bot fir Edward wald never reft,
  Or thai war feld the beft of France.

Of France was mekill wo, i wis,
   And in Paris the high palays:
Now had the bare, with mekill blis,
   Bigged him bifor Calais.
Heres now how the romance fais,
   How fir Edward, oure king with croune,
Held his fege, bi nightes and dais,
   With his men bifor Calays toune.

VII.

HOW EDWARD, ALS THE ROMANCE SAIS, HELD HIS SEGE BIFOR CALAIS.

CALAIS MEN, now may ze care,
    And murning mun ze have to mede;
Mirth on mold get ze no mare,
    Sir Edward fall ken zow zowre crede.
Whilum war ze wight in wede,
    To robbing rathly for to ren;
Mend zow fone of zowre misdede,
    Zowre care es cumen, will ze it ken.

Kend it es how ze war kene
    Al Inglis-men with dole to dere;
Thaire gudes toke ze albidene,
    No man born wald ze forbere;
Ze fpared noght, with fwerd ne fpere,
    To ftik tham, and thaire gudes to ftele;
With wapin and with ded of were,
    Thus have ze wonnen werldes wele.

Weleful men war ze, i wis,
  Bot fer on fold fall ze noght fare,
A bare fal now abate zowre blis,
  And wirk zow bale on bankes bare.
He fall zow hunt als hund dofe hare,
  That in no hole fall ze zow hide;
For all zowre fpeche will he noght fpare,
  Bot bigges him right by zowre fide.

Bifide zow here the bare bigins
  To big his boure in winter-tyde,
And all bityme takes he his ines,
  With femly fergantes him bifide.
The word of him walkes ful wide,
  Jhefu, fave him fro mischance!
In bataill dare he wele habide
  Sir Philip and fir John of France.

The Franche-men er fers and fell,
  And mafe grete dray when thai er dight;
Of tham men herd flike tales tell,
  With Edward think thai for to fight,
Him for to hald out of his right,
  And do him trefon with thaire tales;
That was thaire purpos, day and night,
  Bi counfail of the cardinales.

Cardinales, with hattes rede,
  War fro Calays wele thre myle,
Thai toke thaire counfail in that ftede
  How, thai might fir Edward bigile.
Thai lended thare bot litill while,
  Til Franche-men to grante thaire grace;
Sir Philip was funden a file,
  He fled, and faght noght in that place.

In that place the bare was blith,
  For all was funden that he had foght;
Philip the Valas fled ful fwith,
  With the batail that he had broght:
For to have Calays had he thoght,
  All at his ledeing loud or ftill,
Bot all thaire wiles war for noght,
  Edward wan it at his will.

Lyftens now, and ze may lere,
  Als men the futh may underftand,
The knightes that in Calais were
  Come to fir Edward fare wepeand,
In kirtell one, and fwerd in hand,
  And cried, Sir Edward, thine [we] are,
Do now, lord, bi law of land,
  Thi will with us for evermare.

The noble burgafe and the beft
  Come unto him to have thaire hire;
The comun puple war ful preft
  Rapes to bring obout thaire fwire:
Thai faid all, Sir Philip oure fyre,
  And his fun, fir John of France,
Has left us ligand in the mire,
  And broght us til this doleful dance.

Oure horfes, that war faire and fat,
  Er etin up ilkone bidene,
Have we nowther conig ne cat,
  That thai ne er etin, and hundes kene,
All er etin up ful clene,
  Es nowther levid biche ne whelp,
That es wele on oure fembland fene,
  And thai er fled that fuld us help.

A knight that was of grete renowne,
  Sir John de Viene was his name,
He was wardaine of the toune,
  And had done Ingland mekill fchame.
For all thaire bofte thai er to blame,
  Ful ftalworthly thare have thai ftrevyn,
A bare es cumen to mak tham tame,
  Kayes of the toun to him er gifen.

The kaies er zolden him of the zate,
  Lat him now kepe tham if he kun;
To Calais cum thai all to late,
  Sir Philip and ſir John his ſun:
Al war ful ferd that thare ware fun,
  Thaire leders may thai barely ban.
All on this wiſe was Calais won;
  God ſave tham that it ſo gat wan !

VIII.

Sir David the Brufe
    Was at distance,
When Edward the Baliolfe
    Rade with his lance;
The north end of Ingland
    Teched him to daunce,
When he was met on the more
    With mekill mischance.
Sir Philip the Valayfe
    May him noght avance,
The flowres that faire war
    Er fallen in Fraunce;
The floures er now fallen
    That fers war and fell,
A bare with his bataille
    Has done tham to dwell.

Sir David the Brufe
    Said he fulde fonde
To ride thurgh all Ingland,

Wald he noght wonde;
At the Weſtminſter-hall
  Suld his ſtedes ſtonde,
Whils oure king Edward
  War out of the londe:
Bot now has ſir David
  Mifsed of his merkes,
And Philip the Valays,
  With all thaire grete clerkes.

Sir Philip the Valais,
  Suth for to ſay,
Sent unto ſir David,
  And faire gan him pray,
At ride thurgh Ingland,
  Thaire fomen to ſlay,
And faid none es at home
  To let hym the way;
None letes him the way,
  To wende whore he will:
Bot with ſchiperd-ſtaves
  Fand he his fill.

Fro Philip the Valais
  Was ſir David ſent,
All Ingland to win,

Fro Twede unto Trent;
He broght mani bere-bag,
With bow redy bent;
Thai robbed and thai reved,
And held that thai hent;
It was in the waniand
That thai furth went;
Fro covaitife of cataile
Tho fchrewes war fchent;
Schent war tho fchrewes,
And ailed unfele,
For at the Nevil-cros
Nedes bud tham knele.

At the ersbisfchop of Zork
Now will i bigyn,
For he may, with his right haud,
Asfoyl us of fyn;
Both Dorem and Carlele,
Thai wald nevir blin
The wirfchip of Ingland
With wappen to win;
Mekil wirfchip thai wan,
And wele have thai waken,
For fyr David the Brufe
Was in that tyme taken.

When fir David the Brufe
   Satt on his ftede,
He faid of all Ingland
   Haved he no drede;
Bot hinde John of Coupland,
   A wight man in wede,
Talked to David,
   And kend him his crede:
Thare was fir David
   So dughty in his dede,
The faire toure of Londen
   Haved he to mede.

Sone than was fir David
   Broght unto the toure,
And William the Dowglas,
   With men of honowre;
Full fwith redy fervis
   Fand thai thare a fchowre,
For firft thai drank of the fwete,
   And fenin of the fowre.
Than fir David the Brufe
   Makes his mone,
The faire coroun of Scotland
   Haves he forgone;
He luked furth into France,

Help had he none,
Of fir Philip the Valais,
Ne zit of fir John.

The pride of fir David
  Bigon faft to flaken,
For he wakkind the were
  That held him felf waken;
For Philyp the Valaife
  Had he brede baken,
And in the toure of Londen
  His ines er taken:
To be both in a place
  Thaire forward thai nomen,
Bot Philip fayled thare,
  And David es cumen.

Sir David the Brufe
  On this manere
Said unto fir Philip
  Al thir fawes thus fere :
Philip the Valais,
  Thou made me be here,
This es noght the forward
  We made are to-zere;
Fals es thi forward,

And evyll mot thou fare,
For thou and fir John thi fon
Haves kaft me in care.

The Scottes, with thaire falshede,
Thus went thai obout
For to win Ingland
Whils Edward was out;
For Cuthbert of Dorem
Haved thai no dout,
Tharfore at Nevel-cros
Law gan thai lout;
Thare louted thai law,
And leved allane.
Thus was David the Brufe
Into the toure tane.

IX.

I wald noght ſpare for to ſpeke,
  Wiſt i to ſpede,
Of wight men with wapin,
  And worthly in wede,
That now er driven to dale,
  And ded all thaire dede,
Thai ſail in the ſee-gronde
  Fiſſches to fede;
Fele fiſſches thai fede,
  For all thaire grete fare :
It was in the waniand
  That thai come thare.

Thai ſailed furth in the Swin,
  In a ſomers tyde,
With trompes and taburns,
  And mekill other pride;
The word of tho weremen
  Walked full wide;

The gudes that thai robbed
  In holl gan thai hide;
In holl than thai hided
  Grete welthes, als i wene,
Of gold and of filver,
  Of fkarlet and grene.

When thai failed weftward,
  Tho wight men in were,
Thaire hurdis thaire ankers
  Hanged thai on here;
Wight men of the weft
  Neghed tham nerr,
And gert tham fnaper in the fnare,
  Might thai no ferr;
Fer might thai noght flit,
  Bot thare moft thai fine,
And that thai bifore reved
  Than moft thai tyne.

Boy with thi blac berd,
  I rede that thou blin,
And fone fet the to fchrive,
  With forow of thi fyn;
If thou were on Ingland,
  Noght faltou win,

Cum thou more on that cofte
    Thi bale fall bigin:
Thare kindels thi care,
    Kene men fall the kepe,
And do the dye on a day,
    And domp in the depe.

Ze broght out of Bretayne
    Zowre cuftom with care,
Ze met with the marchandes
    And made tham ful bare;
It es gude refon and right
    That ze evill misfare,
When ze wald in Ingland
    Lere of a new lare:
New lare fall ze lere,
    Sir Edward to lout,
For when ze ftode in zowre ftrenkith
    Ze war all to ftout.

X.

Wᴀʀ this winter oway,
　Wele wald i wene
That fomer fuld fchew him
　In fchawes ful fchene;
Both the lely and the lipard
　Suld geder on a grene.
Mari, have minde of thi man,
　Thou whote wham i mene;
Lady, think what i mene,
　I mak thee my mone;
Thou wreke gude king Edward
　On wikked fyr John.

Of Gynes ful gladly
　Now will i bigin,
We wote wele that woning

Was wikked for to win:
Crift, that fwelt on the rode,
    For fake of mans fyn,
Hald tham in gude hele
    That now er tharein!
Inglis-men er tharein,
    The kastell to kepe;
And John of France es fo wroth
    For wo will he wepe.

Gentill John of Doncaster
    Did a ful balde dede,
When he come toward Gines
    To ken tham thaire crede;
He ftirt unto the castell
    Withowten any ftede,
Of folk that he fand thare
    Haved he no drede;
Dred in hert had he none
    Of all he fand thare;
Faine war thai to fle,
    For all thaire grete fare.

A letherin ledderr,
    'And a lang line,
A fmall bote was tharby,

E

That put tham fro pine;
The folk that thai fand thare
Was faine for to fyne;
Sone thaire diner was dight,
And thare wald thai dine;
Thare was thaire purpofe
To dine and to dwell,
For trefon of the Franche-men,
That fals war and fell.

Say now, fir John of France,
How faltou fare,
That both Calays and Gynes
Has kindeld thi care?
If thou be mán of mekil might,
Lepe up on thi mare,
Take thi gate unto Gines,
And grete tham wele thare;
Thare gretes thi geftes,
And wendes with wo,
King Edward has wonen
The kastell tham fro.

Ze men of Saint-Omers,
Trus ze this tide,
And puttes out zowre paviliownes

With zowre mekill pride;
Sendes efter fir John of Fraunce
　　To ftand by zowre fyde,
A bore es boun zow to biker,
　　That wele dar habide;
Wel dar he habide
　　Bataile to bede,
And of zowre fir John of Fraunce
　　Haves he no drede.

God fave fir Edward his right
　　In everilka nede,—
And he that will noght fo,
　　Evil mot he fpede;—
And len oure fir Edward
　　His life wele to lede,
That he may at his ending
　　Have hevin till his mede.
A M E N.

(•)

ORIGINAL READINGS,

CORRECTED IN THE IMPRESSION.

———

Page 7. Line 9. Skottes.

8.   11. trely.

13.   14. forow and fchame.

14.   19. whe.

         22. mornig.

         23. Igliff.

         24. fhanged.

15.   5. Stalwortly.

         23. fur.

16.   2. feld? ferene.

19.   5. Nomandes.

23.   22. zow.

28.   17. misliling.

30.   20. tyll] toll.

31.   3. murnig.

33.   2. tha.—*As this word has already occured for* the *(see p. 20) it may poffibly be right.*

Page 34. Line 2. murnig.

35. 12. fegantes.

40. 15. flay.

45. 17. werkmen.

46. 2. gan thai it hide.

20. tho.

51. 9. Haveves.

N O T E S.

Page 1.

1. THE BATAILE OF HALIDON-HYLL.] Of this battle (fought the 19th of July 1333) the following particulars are extracted from an old manuscript in the Harleian library (number 4690).

" Att that tyme itte befell thatt king Edwarde of Windefore helde his parlement atte the Newe Caftell uppe Tyne, for diverfe desefes thatt weren in thatt countre; and thenne thider to him come fir Edwarde Bailolle king off Scottelond, and to him he dude homage and feute for the reme off Scottelonde . . . Thanne fir Edward of Bailoll towke his leve off king Edwarde, & went ayenne into Scottelonde, and was fo grete a lorde, & fo moche had his wille, that he touke no hede to hem that halpe him in his quarelle; werefore thei wente thennes fro him & dwelleden in her owne londe, and lyveden with her rentes in Scottelonde. And itte was not longe after thatte the king of Scottelonde wente fro thennes he was at thatt tyme to the towne of Amande *, and ther he towke his

* Annan.

fojourne, and thider comen to him a companie
off knightes & mighty fquieres, & yelde ham
to him, and made him bel continaunce; and fo
thei baren ham to him thatte is trufte was fulliche
in ham : and as fone as the treitours perceiveden
that he trufte on hem, thei asfembled l. orped
men, and wolde have fleine him; butte by the
grace of godde he brake a walle off his chaumber,'
and afcaped her trefoune, as godde wolde; butt
alle his folke werenne yfleye : & fo with grete
paine he come to the towne off Cardoile*, and
there abode, gretely discomforted : and this aven-
ture befelle him in the vigille off the concepcioune
off our lady. And thenne the king of Scottelond
fended to the king of Englonde howgh treitouresly
he was put to fchame in litell wile by his owne
lieges, to the whiche he truftedde gretely; and
therefore he praiedde the king of Englonde, for
the love of godde, thatte he wolde helpe him &
meynteine ayenfte his enemys. Thanne the king
of Englonde, havyng defpyte of that trefoune,
behete him gode focour, and fente to him that he
fchulde holde him in pees in the cete off Cardoille
into the tyme thatte he had gadredde his power.
And thenne king Edwarde of Englond made a
counfeill atte London, & lete asfemble his folke in
diverfe fchires of Englonde, and wente towardo

* Carlile.

the towne of Berwike uppon Twede; and thider
come to him king Edwarde off Scottelonde, with
his power, to befege the towne; and there thei
fette a faire towne & pavylounes, and lete dyche
itte welle alle aboute hem, fo thatte thei hadde no
drede of the Scottes, and made meny asfautes with
gonnes and engines to the town, werewith thei
deftroieden meny menne, & threw a downe many
houfes to the pleine erthe: nottewithftonding, the
Scottes defendedde welle the towne, fo thatte the
king might not come thereynne a grete wile.
But the kingges tweyne befegede the towne fo long
that hem failed vitaile; and alfo thei were fo for-
wacched thatte thei wifte notte watte to do; but
by ther comen asfente thei lette crye on the walles
that thei mighten have pees off Englifchemenne;
and fo thei praiden the kingges off her grace,
and afkeden treues for viii. daies, in thatte cove-
naunt, iff thei werre notte refckewed by the parties of her towne towarde Scottelonde, & off the
Scottes, withynne the fame viii. daies, that thei
fchulde yelde hem, bothe towne & manne, to the
kingges; and to holde that covenaunte thei pro-
ferred the ii. kingges xii. hostages oute off the
towne. Wanne the hoftages weren deliveredde
to the kingges, thei of the towne fenten to the
Scottes to telle hem of her mischieff; and thenne
the Scottes come thider prively, and paffeden the

water of Twede to the bought of goddes houfe;
and fir Willam Dikkette, atte that tyme chieff
ftywarde of Scottelonde, with other Skottes, put
hemfelf in perell off her lyffe atte thatt tyme; for
thei paffeden over the water ther that there ftode
a brigge fom tyme, & the ftones wer coveredde
with the water, and many off her company weren
adreinte; but the forfeide fir Willam paffed over,
& many other off his companie, and come to the
Englifche fchippes; and there in a barge of Hulle
he flowe xvi. menne; and then thei entreden in to
the towne of Berwike bi water. Werefore the
towne helde hem for refckewed, & afkede ayen
her hostages : and the king off Englond fent hem
to feine that thei hafked her hostages with wrong;
for the Scottes entred the towne by the parties off
the towne towarde Englonde, and the covenaunte
was betwene ham that the towne fchulde be res-
kewed towarde the parties of Scottelonde; and
therefore the king commaunded hem to yelde
uppe the towne, or he wolde flee the hostages :
and the Skottes feiden that the towne was res-
kewedde welle ynough; and therto thei wolde
holde ham. Than was the king righte wrothe;
and anone he towke oon off the hostages, that hete
fir Thomas of Seeton, the fone off fir Alifaunder
Seton, wiche was wardeine of Berwikke; and this
fir Thomas was parfon off Dunbar; and he towke

him firſte of alle the hoſtages * ; and then the king
ſente hem worde thatt every day he wolde take
too off the hoſtages, and do to ham alle the deſs-
eſſe that he mighte, if thei wolde not yelde him
the town ; and ſo he wolde teche hem to kepe
her covenauntz. And whan thei off the towne
herd theſe tidingges, thei were wonder ſory, and
ſenten ayenne to the king off Englonde, prayynge
him to graunte hem other viii. daies off reſpite,
with ſoche covenaunte, thatt iff ii.c. men of armes
might paſſe by hem & entre in to the towne bi
ſtrengthe, to vitaille ham, thatte thanne the towne
ſchulde be holde reſkewedde ; and iff xxi. or xxii.
or mo weren ſleye off the ii.c. before ſeide, that
the town ſchulde notte be holde reſkewedde :
and to this the king accordedde, & towke other
xii. hostages. And in the mene wile, on ſeinte
Margareteis eve, in the yere off grace a mˡ. ccc. &
' xxxiii.' the Scottes come oute off Scottelonde
ferſly, in iiii. wingges, welle araied in armour,
to mete with king Edwarde of Englond and king
Edwarde off Scottelonde with a grete power
aboute even-ſong tyme. And at that ſam tyme
was a grete flode on the water off Twede, that
no man might paſſe that water on horſe ne on
fote, & that water was betwene Englond and the

---

* *Subintelligitur*—and hanged him. The execution took
place in the fathers fight.

ii. kingges ; & then the Scottes aboden, hoping
that by her ftrengthe the Englifchemen fchulden
be flaine with fighting, or elles be adreinte; but,
worfchipped be god, the falfe Scottes faileden off
her purpofe . . . . The erle of Dunbar, keper of
the castell of Berwikke, halpe the Scottes with l.
men off armes. Sir Alifaunder Seton, keper off
the town of Berwike, halpe the Scottes with an
hundred men off armes : and the comens off the
town with iiii.c. men of armes, x.mˡ. & viii.c.
fote menne. The fom of erles & lordes amownteth
lxv. The fom off bachelers newe dubbed, a c. &
xl. The fom off men off armes, iii.mˡ. vi.c. xlᵗˡ.
The fom of comineres, iiii.fcore mˡ. & ii.c. The
fom total off alle the pepelle amownteth, iiiiˣˣmˡ.
xv.m. & v.c. & v.* And thes forfeide lxv. grete
lordes, with iiii. bateilles, as it is before defcri-
vedde, come alle afote; and king Edwarde off
Englonde and king Edwarde off Skottelonde had
well pairaled her folke in iiii. bateilles on fote,
alfo to fighte ayenfte her enemys. And then the
Englifche mynftrelles beten her tabers, & blewen
her trompes, and pipers pipeden loude, and made
a grete fchoute uppon the Skottes. And then
hadde the Englifche bachelers eche off hem ii.
wingges off archers, which atte thatte meting
mightly drewen her bowes, & made arowes flee

---

* Thefe numbers appear to be inaccurate.

as thik as motes on the fonne beme; and fo theie
fmote the Skottes that thei fell to grounde by
many m¹. and anone the Skottes beganne to flee
fro the Englifchemenne, to fave ther lyves. Butt
wanne the knaves & the Skottifche pages, that
weren behinde the Skottes to kepe her horfes,
feyen the discomfiture, thei prikeden her maisters
horfes awey to kepe hemfelfe from perelle; and
fo thei towke no hede off her maisters. And
then the Englifchemen towken many off the
Skottes horfes, and prikeden after the Skottes,
& flewe hem downerighte: and there men mighte
fee the nowbell king Edwarde off Englonde, &
his folke, hough mannefully thei chafeden the
Skottes; weroff this romance was made.

THERE men mighte well fee
Many a Skotte lightely flee,
And the Englifche after priking,
With fcharpe fwerdes them ftriking,
And there her baners weren founde,
Alle displayedde on the grounde,
And layne ftarkly on blode,
As thei had fought on the flode.
Butt the Skottes, ille mote thei thee!
Thought the Englifch adreint fchulde be,
For bicaufe thei mighte not flee,
Butte iff thei adreinte fchulde bee.

Butte thei kepte hem manly on londe,
So thatte the Scottes might nott ftonde,
And felde hem downe to grounde,
Many thowfandes in thatte ftounde ;
And the Englifchemen purfuyed hem fo
Tille the flode was alle agoo.
Alle thus the Skottes discomfite were
In littell tyme with grete feere.
For non other wife dide thei ftryve
But as xx. fchepe among wolfes fyve;
For v. off hem then were
Ayenfte an Englifchman there :
So there itte was welle femyug
That with multitude is no fcomfiting ;
But with god, fulle of mighte,
Wham he will helpe in trewe fighte.
So was this, bi goddes grace,
Discomfiture off Skottes in that place,
That men cleped Halidown-hille,
For there this bateill befelle,
Atte Berwike befide the towne
This was do with mery fowne,
With pipes, trompes, and nakers therto,
And loude clariounes thei blew alfo.
And there the Scottes leyen dede,
xxx.m^l. beyonde Twede,
& v.m^l. tolde thereto,
With vii.c.xii. and mo ;

& of Englifchemen but fevenne,
Worfchipped be god in hevenne!
& that wer men on fote goyng,
By foly of her owne doyng.
On feinte Margeteys eve, as y yow tell,
Befille the victory of Halidoune-hille,
In the yere of god almightè
A mˡ.iii.c. and ' iii.' and thritty.
Atte this discomfiture
The Englifch knightes towke her hure
Of the Skottes that weren dede,
Clothes & haberjounes for her mede;
And watteever thei might finde
On the Skottes thei lefte not behinde;
And the knaves, by her purchas,
Hadde there a mery folas,
For thei hadde, for her degree,
In alle her lyffe the better to be.
Alle thus the bateille towke ending;
But y canne not telle off the yen going
Off the too kingges, were thei become,
& wether thei wenten out or home:
But godde, thatte is heven king,
Sende us pees and gode ending!"

The Englifh historians are thought to have ex-
aggerated the number and carnage of the enemy.
They are compared by one old author to a fwarm

of locufts, and their lofs, in killed, is generàlly
ftated at upward of thirty thoufand. "He flewe
of them," fays Fabian, " as testifieth divers writers, feven earles, nine hundred knightes and ba-
nerettes, foure hundred efquiers, and upon thirty
two thoufand of the common people; and of Englifhmen were flaine but onely fiftene perfons."—
Froisfart has a chapter upon the fiege of Berwick,
but takes not the leaft notice of this great and
bloody battle.

Page 4.

L. 4. *Of wild Scottes, and alls of tame.*] Thefe
"wild Scottes " were the inhabitants of the high-
lands and weftern iles, of Galloway, and other
parts ; thofe, in fhort, who adhered to the ancient
drefs or manners, and Irifh or Piçtifh language.
The "tame" Scots, of courfe, were the low-
landers, who fpoke Englifh.

L. 10. *At Dondé now es done thaire daunce.*] The
authors allufion is to the battle of Duplin, (a village in the neighbourhood of Perth,) fought the
12th of Auguft 1332, in which an army of forty
thoufand Scots, under the command of Donald
earl of Mar, regent, (who was flain in the conflict,) were completely and disgracefully overthrown, with great eafe, and prodigious flaughter, by Edward Baliol, and the disinherited Englifh barons, (fuch, that is, as had loft their Scot-

tifh posfesfions) with their followers, to the amount
of about three thoufand men. Duplin, however,
is at a confiderable distance from Dundee; but
the engagement might have obtained a name from
the latter place, by reafon of Baliols fleet being
ftationed there; he and his forces having been pre-
vioufly landed at Kinghorn. See the "Annals
of Scotland," by lord Hailes.

L. 21. *Sir Jon the Comyn*, &c.] Sir John Comyn of Badenoch, a powerful Scotifh baron, in
the Englifh intereft, was flain by Robert Bruce,
afterward king of Scotland, at a private conference between them, in the friery-church, Dumfries, on the 10th of February 1305-6. The immediate motive to this act of violence has not
tranfpired; though historians feem as confident
in their guefses as if they had been actually prefent at the interview.

Page 6.

II. [THE] BATAYL OF BANOCBURN.] This
battle was fought on the 24th of June 1314, between the Englifh and Scotifh armies, headed by
their refpective fovereigns (Edward II. and Robert Bruce); in which the Englifh were completely defeated. Bannockburn is in the fhire of
Stirling.

Saint-Johnes-toune.] Perth, of which Baliol took
posfesfion the day after the battle of Duplin.

Page 8.

III. How Edward the king come in Braband,

And toke homage of all the land.]
" The kyng of Englande," according to Froisfart, whofe relation is here tranfcribed, " made
great purveyances; and whan the wynter was
pafsed he toke the fee, well acompanyed with
dukes, erles, and barownes, and dyvers other
knyghtes; and aryved at the towne of Andewarpe, as than pertayninge to the duke of Brabant. Thyther came people from all partes to
fe hym, and the great eftate that he kept. Than
he fent to his cofyn the duke of Brabant, and to
the duke of Guerles; to the marques of Jullers, to
the lorde Johan of Heynalt, and to all fuch as he
trufted to have any conforte of; fayng howe he
wolde gladly fpeke with theym : they came all to
Andewarpe bytwene Whytfontyde and the feeft
of faynte Johan. And whan the kyng had well
feafted them, he defyred to knowe their myndes,
whanne they wolde begynne that they had promyfed; requirynge them to dyfpatche the mater
brevely; for that intente, he fayd, he was come
thyder, and had all his men redy: and howe it
fhulde be a great damage to hym to deferre the
mater long. Thefe lordes had longe counfell
among them, and fynally they fayd: Syr, our

commynge hyther as nowe was more to fe you
than for any thynge els: we be nat as nowe pur-
veyed to gyve you a ful anfwere. By your lycence, we fhall retourne to our people, and cume
agayne to you at your pleafure; and thanne gyve
you fo playne an anfwere that the mater fhall nat
reft in us. Than they toke day to come agayn a
thre wekes after the feeft of faynt John . . . So
thus thefe lordes departed, and the kynge taryed
in the abbay of faynt Brunarde, and fome of the
Englyffhe lordes taryed ftyll at Andewarpe, to
kepe the kynge company, and fome of the other
rode about the countrey in great dyfpence . . .
The day came that the kynge of Englande loked
to have an anfwere of thefe lordes; and they ex-
cufed them, and fayd howe they were redy and
their men, fo that the duke of Brabant wolde be
redy for his part; fayeng that he was nere than
they . . . Than the kyng dyd fo muche that he
fpake agayne with the duke, and fhewed him the
anfwere of the other lordes, defyring him by amyte
and lynage that no faut were founde in him; fayeng how he parceyved well that he was but cold
in the mater; and that, without he wer quicker,
and dyd otherwife, he douted he fhulde lefe ther-
by the ayde of all the other lordes of Almayne
through his defaulte. Than the duke fayd, he
wolde take counfayle in the matter; and whan he

had longe debated the mater, he fayd he fhulde
be as redy as any other; but firfte, he fayd, he
wolde fpeke agayne with the other lordes; and he
dyde fende for them, defyring them to come to
hym wher as they pleafed beft. Than the day
was apointed about the myddes of Auguft, & this
counfell to be at Hale, bycaufe of the yong erle
of Haynalt, who fhulde alfo be ther, and with
hym fir Johan of Heinalt his uncle. Whann thefe
lordes were all come to this parlyament at Hale,
they had longe counfayle togyder; finally they
fayd to the kyng of Englande: Syr, we fe no
caufe why we fhulde make defyance to the Frenche
kyng, all thynges confydred, without ye can
gette thagrement of themperour; and that he
wolde commaunde us to do fo in his name. The
emperour may well thus do, for of long tyme
paft there was a covenant fworne and fealed that
no kyng of Fraunce ought to take any thyng
parteyning to thempyre, and this kynge Phylippe
hath taken the caftell of Crevecure in Cambreyfis,
and the caftell of Alves in Pailleull, and the cytie
of Cambray: wherfore themperour hath good
caufe to defye hym by us; therfore, fir, if ye
can get his acord, our honour fhal be the more :
and the kyng fayd he wolde folowe their counfayle. Than it was ordayned that the marques
of Jullers fhulde go to themperour, and certayne

knyghtes and clarkes of the kynges, and fome of
the counfell of the duke of Gwerles. But the
duke of Brabant woulde fend none fro hym;
but he lende the caftell of Lovayne to the kynge
of Englande to lye in. And the marques and his
company founde the emperour at Florebetche,
and fhewed hym the caufe of their commyng.
And the lady Margarete of Heynault dydde all
her payne to further forthe the mater, whom fir
Lewes of Bavyer than emperour had wedded . . .
And themperour gave commysfion to four knyghtes
and to two doctours of this counfell to make kyng
Edwarde of Englande his vycarre generall throughout al the empyre; and therof thefe fayd lordes
hadde inftrumentes publyke, confyrmed and fealed fuffyciently by the emperour . . . And than
about the feeft of all fayntes the marques of Jullers and his company fent worde to the kyng how
they had fped. And the kyng fent to hym that
he fhulde be with hym about the feeft of faynt
Martyne; and alfo he fent to the duke of Brabant to knowe his mynde, wher he wolde the parlyament fhuld be holde; and he anfwered at Ar-
ques, in the county of Loz, nere to his countrey.
And than the kyng fent to all other of his alyes,
that they fhulde be there; and fo the hal of the
towne was apparelled and hanged, as though it
hat ben the kynges chamber. And there the

kyng fatte crowned with geolde v. fote hygher
than any other: and there openly was rede the
letters of themperour, by the which the kyng
was made vycare generall and lieftenaunt for the
emperour, and had power gyven hym to make
lawes, and to mynistre justyce to every perfon in
themperours name, and to make money of golde
and fylver. The emperour alfo there commaunded
by his letters, that all perfons of his empyre, and
all other his fubgiettes fhulde obey to the kyng of
England his vycare as to hymfelfe, and to do hym
homage . . . And whan all this was done the
lordes departed, and toke day that they fhulde all
appere before Cambray thre wekes after the feeft
of faynt Johan, the whiche towne was become
Frenche: thus they all departed, and every man
went to his owne." (Froisfarts chronicle, translated by fir John Bourchier lord Berners, 1525,
fo. b. l. volume i. chap. 32, 34.)

Page 9.

L. 15. *And thare be made his moné playne.*]
"Kynge Edwarde, as vycare of thempyre, went
then to Lovayne to the quene, who was newly
come theyder out of England, with great noble-
neffe, and well accompanyed with ladyes and do-
mofels of Englande. So there the kynge and the
quene kepte their houfe ryght honorably all that
wynter; and caufeed money, golde and fylver,

to be made at Andewarpe, great plentie." (Froisfarts chronicle.)

Page 10.

L. 3. *Schip-men fone war efter fent*, &c.] "The
Frenche kynge on his part had fet Genowayes,
Normans, Bretons, Pycardes, and Spanyardes, to
be redy on the fee to entre into Englande asfone
as the warre were opened." (Froisfart, vol. i.
c. 35.)

L. 13. *At Hamton*, &c.] "Asfone as fir Hewe
Quyriell, [r. Quyriett] fir Peter Babuchet, and
Barbe Noyre, who lay and kept the ftreightes
'bytwene' England and Fraunce with a great navy, knewe that the warre was opyn, they came
on a fonday in the forenoone to the havyn of
Hampton, whyle the people were at maffe; and
the Normayns, Pycardes, and Spanyerdes entred
into the towne, and robbed and pylled the towne,
and flewe dyvers, and defowled maydens, and en-
forced wyves, and charged their veffels with that
pyllage; and fo entred agayne into their fhyppes :
and whan the tyde came they disancred, and fayled
to Normandy, and came to Depe; and there departed and devyded their boty and pyllages."
(Froisfart, vol. i. chap. 37.)

L. 25. *The galay-men*, &c.] "Kyng Philyppe,"
fays Froisfart, "greatly fortyfyed his navy that
he hadde on the fee, wherof fyr [Hewe] Kiry[ett],

[fir Peter] Bahuchet, and Barbe Noyre were cap-
taines: and they had under them a great retinue
of Genowaies, Normayns, Bretons, and Picardes.
They dyd that wynter great domage to the realme
of England. Somtyme they came to Dover, Sand-
wyche, Winchelfe, Haftinges, and Rye: and did
moche forowe to thenglifhemen, for the were a
great nombre, as a xl. m. men. Ther was none
that coude ysfue out of England, but they were
robbed, taken or flayne: fo they wan great pyllage, and fpecyally they wan a great fhype called
Christofer, laden with wolles, as fhe was goyng into
Flaunders; the whiche fhype had cofte the kyng
of England much money; and all they that were
taken within the fhippe were fleine and drowned:
of the which conqueft the Frenchemen wer right
joyoufe." (Chap. 44.)

The account given of this affair by Fabian is
more particular than Froisfarts.

" In the xiii. yeare [1338], kynge Edward with
quene Philip hys wyfe, for moore asfured ftablifh-
ment of amitie, to be had betwene him and the
Hollanders, Sealanders, and Brabanders, pasfed
the fea in the beginninge of the moneth of ' Ju-
lye,' & fayled with a goodly companye into the
countrey of Brabant, the queene then being great
with childe, where of the earle of Brabant he was
honorably receaved, &c. . . . . In this paffetyme,

the Frenche king had fent dyvers fhyppes unto the
fea with men of warre, for to take the Englyfhe
marchauntes and other that came in theyr courfe.
And fo befell that they encountred with two great
fhippes of England, called the Edwarde and the
Christopher, the whiche (as testifieth the French
chronicle) were freyt with great riches, and alfo
well manned. Anone, as either was ware of other,
gonnes, and fhot of longe bowes, and arblasters,
were not fpared on nother fide, fo that betwene
them was a cruell fyght, but not egall: for of
the French men wer xiii. failes great and fmal, &
of the Englifhmen but five, that is to meane, thefe
two forefaid great fhips, two barckes and a carvell,
the which thre fmal fhips, efcaped by their deliver
fayling, and the two abode & fought beyonde ix.
houres, fo much that there were flaine upon bothe
parties above fixe hundred men; but, in the end,
the faid two fhips wer taken, and brought into the
French kinges ftreames, & many of the Englyfhmen
that were wounded caft into the fea." (P. 206.)

Page 13.

L. 21. *Furth he ferd into France*, &c.] " Asfone
as kyng Edward had pasfed the river of Lefcaute *,
and was entred into the realme of Fraunce, he . . .
went and lodged in thabbey of mount faint Martyn, and there taryed two dayes, and his people

* The Scheld.

abode in the countrey, & the duke of Brabant
was lodged in thabbey of Vancelliz . . . And the
next day on the mornyng the kyng departed from
Mount Saynt Martyn . . . and fo than they entred
into Vermandoys, and toke that day their lodgyng
be tymes on the mount Saynt Quintyne in good
order of batayle . . . Than the lordes toke counfell what way they fhulde drawe, and, by thadvyce
of the duke of Brabant, they toke the way to Thy-
eraffe, for that way their provifyon came dayly to
them. And they determyned that if kyng Phy-
lyppe dyd followe them, as they fuppofed he wolde
do, that than they wolde abyde hym in the plane
felde, and gyve hym batayle. Thus they went
forthe in thre great batayls: the marfhalles and
the Almaygnes had the firft, the kynge of Englande in the myddle warde, & the duke of Brabant in the rerewarde. Thus they rodde forthe,
brennynge and pyllynge the countrey a thre or
foure leages a day, and ever toke their logynge
betymes. And a company of Englyffhmen and
Almaygnes pafsed the ryver of Somme, by the
abbey of Vermans, and wafted the countrey al
about. An other company, wherof fir Johan of
Heynault, the lord Faulquemont, and fir Arnold
of Bacquehen were chefe, rode to Origny Saint
Benoyfte, a good towne; but it was but eafely
clofed: incontynent it was taken by asfaut, and

robbed, and an abbey of ladyes vyolated, and the
towne brent. Than they departed, and rode towarde Guys and Rybemont, and the kynge of
Englande lodged at Vehories, and ther taryed a
day, and his men ranne abrode, and dyſtroyed the
countrey. Than the kynge toke the way to the
Flammengerie, to come to Leſche in Thyeraſſe,
and the marſhals and the bysſhoppe of Lincolne
with a fyve hundered ſperes paſſed the ryver of
Tryſague, and entred into Laonnoys, towarde
the lande of the lorde of Coucey, and brent Saynt
Gouven, and the towne of Marle. And on a
nyght lodgedde in the valley beſyde Laon, and
the nexte day they drewe agayne to their hooſt;
for they knewe by ſome of their priſoners, that
the Frenche kyng was come to Saynt Quyntines
with a c. thouſand men, and there to paſſe the ryver of Somme. So theſe lordes in their return-
ynge brent a good towne called Crecy, and dyverſe other townes and hamelettes therabout . . .
The kynge of Englande departed fro Sarnaques
and went to Muttrell; and ther loged a nyght;
and the next day he went to the Flamengery, and
made all his men to loge nere about hym, wherof
he had mo than xl. thouſande; and there he was
counſelled to abyde kyng Philyp, and to fyght with
hym. The French kyng departed fro Saynt Quyntines; and dayly men came to him fro all partes,

and fo came to Vyronfoſſe. There the kyng taryed, & ſayd howe he wold nat go thens tyll he
had fought with the kynge of Englande, and with
his alyes, ſeyng they were within two leages to-
guyther . . . Thus theſe two kynges were lodged
bytwene Vyronfoſſe and Flamengery, in the playne
feldes, without any advauntage. I thynke ther was
never ſen before ſo goodly an aſſemble of noble men
togyder as was there. Whanne the kynge of England, beyng in the chapell of Thyeraſſe, knewe how
that king Philyppe was within two leages, than he
called the lordes of his hoſt togyder, and demaunded of them what he ſhuld do, his honour ſaved,
for he ſayd that his entencyon was to gyve batayle. Than the lordes behelde eche other, and
they deſyredde the duke of Brabant to ſhewe firſt
his entent. The duke ſayd that he was of the accorde that they ſhulde gyve batayle, for otherwyſe,
he ſayd, they coude nat depart, ſavyng their ho-
nours; wherfore he counſayled that they ſhulde
ſende herauldes to the Frenche kyng, to demaunde
a day of batayle. Than an heraulde of the duke
of Guerles, who coude well the langage of Frenche,
was enformed what he ſhulde ſay, and ſo he rode
tyll he came in to the Frenche hooſt. And 'than'
he drewe hym to kyng Philyppe and to his counſayle; and ſayde, Sir, the kynge of Englande is
in the felde, and deſyreth to have batell, power

agaynſt power : the whiche thyng kyng Philyppe
graunted, and toke the day, the Friday next after; and as than it was Wedniſday. And ſo the
haraude retourned, well rewarded with good fur-
red gownes gyven hym by the French kyng and
other lordes, bycauſe of the tidynges that he
brought. So thus the journey was agreed, &
knowledge was made therof to all the lordes of
bothe the hooſtes, and ſo every man made hym
redy to the mater . . . Whan the Friday came in
the mornyng, both hooſtes aparelled themſelfe
redy, and every lorde harde maſſe among their
owne companyes, and dyvers wer ſhriven. · Firſt
we woll ſpeke of thorder of thenglyſſhmen, who
drewe them forwarde into the felde, and made
iii. batels a fote, and dyd put al their horſes and
bagages into a lytell wood behynde them, and for-
tefyed it. The firſt batel ledde the duke of Guerles, the marques of Nuſſe, the marquyes of Blan-
quebure, ſir Johan of Heynault, therle of Mons,
therle of Savynes, the lorde of Faulquemont, ſir
Guyllam du Fort, ſir Arnolde of Baquehen, and
the Almayns; and amonge them was xxii. ban-
ners, and lx. penons in the hole, and viii.m. men.
The ſeconde batayle had the duke of Brabant, and
the lordes and knyghtes of his countrey . . . The
duke of Brabant had xxiiii. baners, and lxxx.
penons, and in al vii.m. men. The iii. batayle

& the gretteſt had the kyng of Englande, and
with hym his coſyn therle of Derby *, the bysſhoppe of Lynecolne, the bysſhoppe of Durame,
therle of Saliſbury, the erle of Northampton and
of Glocetter, therle of Suffolke, ſir Robert Dartoyſe, as than called erle of Rychmont, the lorde
Raynolde Cobham, the lorde Perſy, the lorde
Rooſe, the lord Montbray, ſir Lewes and ſir Johan
Beauchampe, the lord Dalawarre, the lorde of
Laucome, the lorde Basſet, the lorde Fitzwater,
ſir Water Manny, ſir Hewe Haſtynges, ſir Johan
Lyle; and dyvers other that I can nat name,
among other was ſir Johan Chandos, of whom
moche honour is ſpoken in this boke. The kyng
had with hym xxviii. baners, and lxxxx. penons, and in his batale a vi.m. men of armes, and
vi.m. archers; and he had ſet an other batell as
in a wyng, wherof therle of Warwyke, therle of
Penbroke, the lorde Barkly, the lorde Multon,
and dvyerſe other were as cheyſe, and they were
on horsbacke. Thus, whan every lorde was under his banner, as it was commaunded by the marſhals, the kyng of England mounted on a palfray,
acompanyed all onely with ſir Robert Dartoyſe,
ſir Raynolde Cobham, and ſir Water of Manny,
and rode along before all his batels, and right
ſwetely deſyred all his lordes and other, that they

* Afterward duke of Lancaster.

wolde that day ayde to defende his honoure; and
they all promyfed hym fo to do. Than he returned
to his owne batell, and fet every thing in good
order, and commaunded that non fhuld go before
the marfhals baners.

" Nowe let us fpeke of the lordes of Fraunce
what they dyd. They were xi. fcore baners,
iiii. kynges, v. dukes, xxvi. erles, and mo than
iiii.m. knyghtes; and of the commons of Fraunce
mo than lx.m. The kynges that were there with
kyng Philyppe of Valoys, was the kyng ' of Behayne,' the kyng of Naverre, and kyng Davyd of
Scotland; the duke of Normandy, the duke of
Bretayne, the duke of Bourbon, the duke of Lor-
rayne, and the duke of Athenes. Of erles: therle
of Alanfon, ' brother' to the kyng, the erle of
Flaunders, therle of Heynalt, the erle of Bloys,
therle of Bare, therle of Foreftes, therle of Foyz,
therle of Armynack, the erle Dophym of Au-
vergne, therle of Vandofme, therle of Harrecourt,
therle of Saynt Pol, therle of Guynes, therle of
Bowlongne, therle of Rousfy, therle of Dampmar-
tyn, therle of Valentynois, therle of Aucer, therle
of Saucerre, therle of Genue, the erle of Dreux
and of Gafcongue, and of Languedoc. So many
erles and vycuntes that it were longe to reherfe.
It was a great beauty to beholde the baners and
ftandredes, wavyng in the wynde; and horfes

barded; and knyghtes and fquyers richely armed. The Frenchemen ordayned thre great batayls; in eche of them fyftene thoufand men of armes, [and] xx.m. men a fote.

" It myght well be marveyledde, howe fo goodly a fight of men of warre, fo nere togyder, fhulde depart without batayle. But the French-men were nat al of one accorde, they were of dy-vers opynyons. Some fayde, it were a great fhame and they fought nat, feyng their ennemys fo nere them, in their owne countre, raynged in the felde; and alfo had promyfed to fyght with them. And fome other fayd, it fhulde be a great folly to fyght, for it was harde to knowe every mannes mynde, and jeopardy of treafon. For, they fayd, if for-tune were contrary to their kyng, as to lefe the felde, he than fhuld put all his hole realme in a jeopardy to be loft; and though he dyd dysconfet his ennemes, yet for all that he fhuld be never the nerer of the realme of Englande, nor of fuch landes parteynyng to any of thofe lordes that be with hym alyed. Thus, in ftrivyng of dyvers opynions, the day paft tyll it was paft noone; and then fo-denly there ftarted an hare among the French-men; and fuch as fawe her cryed and made gret brunt, wherby fuche as were behynde thought they before had ben fightynge, and fo put on their helmes, and toke their fperes in their handes: and fo there were made dyvers newe knyghtes; and fpecially therle of Heynalt made xiiii. who were ever after called knyghtes of the hare. Thus that batell ftode ftyll all that Friday. And befyde this ftryfe bytwene the counfellours of France, there was brought in letters to the hooft, of recommen- dacion to the Frenche kyng, and to his counfell, fro kyng Robert of Cicyle; the which kyng, as it was fayd, was a great aftronomyre, and full of great fcience. He had oftentymes fought his bokes on the ftate of the kynges of England and France; and he founde by his aftrology, and by thenfluens of the hevens, that if the French kyng ever fought with kyng Edwarde of England, he fhuld be disconfited: wherfore he, lyke a king of gret wysdome, and as he that douted the peryll of the Frenche kyng his cofyn, fent oftentymes' letters to king Philyppe, and to his counfayle, that in no wyfe he fhulde make any batayle agaynft thenglyffhmen, where as kyng Edwarde was per- fonally prefent. So that, what for dout, and for fuch writyng fro the king of Cecyle, dyvers of the great lordes of Fraunce were fore abaffhed; and alfo kynge Philyppe was enfourmed therof. Howebeit yet he had great wyll to gyve batayle, but he was fo counfelled to the contrary, that the day pafsed without batell, and every man with- drue to their lodgynges. And whan the erle of

G

Heynalt fawe that they fhuld nat fight, he departed with all his hole company, and went backe
the fame night to Quesnoy. And the kynge of
Englande, the duke of Brabant, and all the other
lordes, returned and trufsed all their bagagis, and
went the fame night to Davefnes in Heynalt. And
the next day they toke leve eche of other; and
the Almayns and Brabances departed, and the
kynge went into Brabant with the duke his cofyn. The fame Friday that the batell fhulde have
ben, the French kynge, whan he came to his lodgyng, he was fore dyspleafed, bycaufe he departed
without batayle. But thay of his counfayle fayde,
howe right nobly he had borne hymfelfe, for he
had valyantly purfued his enemies, and had done
. fo muche that he had put them out of his realme;
and how that the kyng of England fhulde make
many fuch vyages or he conquered the realme of
Fraunce. The next day kyng Philyppe gave
lycence to all maner of men to depart, and he
thanked right courtesly the gret lordes of their
ayde and focour. Thus ended this great journey; and every man went to theyr owne." Froisfart, vol i. chap. 39, &c. This was in 1339.

Page 18.

V. L<small>ITHES</small>, AND THE BATTAIL I SAL BEGYN
OF I<small>NGLISSH</small> MEN AND NORMANDES IN
THE S<small>WYN</small>.]

" Nowe lette us ... fpeke of the kynge of Englande, who was on the fee to the intent to arryve
in Flaunders, and fo into Heynalt to make warre
agaynft the Frenchmen. This was on Mydfomer
even, in the yere of our lord m.ccc.xl. all then-
glyffe flete was departed out of the ryver of Tames,
and toke the way to Slufe. And the fame tyme
bytwene Blanqueberque and Slufe on the fee was
fir Hewe ' Kyryett,' fir Peter Bahuchet, and Barb-
noyr : and mo than fix fcore great vesfels befyde
other, and they were of Normayns, Bydaulx, Ge-
nowes, and Pycardes; about the nombre of xl.m.
There they were layd by the Frenche kyng, to defende the kyng of England pasfage. The kynge
of England and his came faylyng tyll he came before Slufe; and whan he fawe fo great a nombre of
fhippes that their maftes femed to be lyke a great
wood, he demaunded of the mayster of his fhip
what peple he thought they were; he anfwered
and fayde, Sir, I thynke they be Normayns layd
here by the Frenche kynge; & hath done gret
dyspleafure in Englande, brent your towne of
Hamton, and taken your great fhyppe the Chrys-
tofer. A, quod the kinge, I have longe defyred to

fyght with the Frenchemen, and nowe fhall I
fyght with fome of them, by the grace of god
and faynt George, for truly they have done me
fo many dyfplefurs that I fhall be revenged & I
may. Than the king fet all his fhyppes in order,
the gretteft before, well furniffhed with archers,
& ever bytwene two fhyppes of archers he had
one fhypp with men of armes, and than he made
an other batell to ly a lofe with archers to confort
ever them that were mooft wery, yf nede were.
And there were a great nombre of countefses, ladyes, knyghtes wyves, & other damofels that were
goyng to fe the quene at Gaunt: thefe ladyes
the kyng caufed to be well kept with thre hundred men of armes, and v.c. archers.

 " Whan the kyng and his marfhals had ordered his batayls, he drewe up the feales and cam
with a greater wynde, to have the vauntage of
the fonne. And fo at laft they tourned a lytell to
get the wynde at wyll: and whan the Normayns
fawe them recule backe, they had marvell why
they dyde fo. And fome fayd, They thinke them
felfe nat mete to medyll with us; wherfore they
woll go backe. They fawe well howe the kyng
of England was there perfonally, by reafon of his
baners. Than they dyd appareyle their flet in
order, for they wer fage and good men of ware
on the fee; and dyd fet the Chriftofer, the which

they had won the yer before, to be formaſt with
many trumpettes and inſtrumentes : and ſo ſet on
their ennemies. There began a ſore batell on
bothe partes : archers and crosbowes began to
ſhote, and men of armes aproched and foughte
hande to hande; and the better to come togyder,
they had great hokes, & grapers of yron to caſt
out of one ſhyppe into another, and ſo tyed them
faſt togyder. There were many dedes of armes
done, takyng and rescuyng agayne. And at laſt
the great Christopher was firſt won by thenglyſſhmen, and all that were within it taken or ſlayne.
Than there was great noyſe and cry, and thenglyſſhmen aproched and fortifyed the Christofer
with archers, and made hym to paſſe on byfore
to fyght with the Genoweys. This batayle was
right fierſe and terryble ; for the batayls on the
ſee ar more dangerous and fierſer than the batayls by lande : for on the ſee ther is no reculyng
nor fleyng, there is no remidy but to fight, and to
abyde fortune, and every man to ſhewe his prowes.
Of a trouthe ſir Hewe ' Kyriett,' and ſir [Peter]
Bahuchet, and Barbe-noyer were ryght good and
expert men of warre. This batayle endured fro
the mornyng tyll it was noone, & thenglyſſhmen
endured moche payne, for their ennemies were
foure agaynſt one, and all good men on the ſee.
Ther the kyng of England was a noble knight of

his owne handes, he was in the flouer of his yougli. In like wyſe ſo was the erle of Derby, Pembroke, Herforde, Huntyngdon, Northampton, and Glocetter, ſir Raynolde Cobham, ſir Rycharde Stafforde, the lorde Percy, ſir Water of Manny, ſir Henry of Flaunders, ſir Johan Beauchamp, the lorde Felton, the lorde Braſſeton, ſir [John] Chandos, the lorde Delawarre, the lorde of Multon, ſir Robert Dartoys, called erle of Rychmont, and dyverſe other lordes and knyghtes, who bare themſe[l]fe ſo valyantly, with ſome ſocours that they had of Bruges, and of the countrey thereabout, that they obtayned the vyctorie. So that the Frenchmen, Normayns, and other were dysconfetted, ſlayne, and drowned: there was nat one that ſcaped, but all were ſlayne. Whane this vyctorie was atchyved, the kyng all that nyght abode in his ſhyppe before Sluſe, with great noyſe of trumpettes and other inſtrumentes. Thyder came to ſe the kynge dyvers of Flaunders, ſuche as had herde of the kynges commyng, &c." Froiſſart, vol. i. c. 50.

"The French king being advertiſed that the king of England meant ſhortlie to returne into Flanders with a great power, in purpoſe to invade the realme of France on that ſide, asſembled a navie of foure hundred ſhippes under the leading of three expert capteins of the warres by ſea, as

fir Hugh Kiriell [r. Kiriett], fir Peter Bahuchet,
and a Geneweis named Barbe-noir, appointing
them to the coafts of Flanders to defend the king
of England from landing there, if by any meanes
they might. Thefe three capteins or admerals
came and laie with their fhips in the haven of
Sluife, for that it was fuppofed the king of England would arrive there, as his meaning was indeed. Whereupon, when his men, fhips, and pro-
vifions were once readie, in the moneth of June
[1340], he tooke the fea with two hundred faile,
and directing his courfe towards Flanders, there
came unto him the lord Robert Morley, with the
north navie of England, fo that then he had in all
about three hundred faile, or (as other faie) two
hundred and three fcore.

" The French navie laie betwixt Sluife and
Blancbergh, fo that when the king of England
approched, either part defcried other, & therewith prepared them to batell. The king of England ftaied, till the funne, which at the firft was in
his face, came fomewhat weftward, and fo had it
upon his backe, that it fhould not hinder the fight
of his people, and fo therewith did fet upon his
enimies with great manhood, who likewife verie
ftoutly incountered him, by reafon whereof in-
fued a fore and deadlie fight betwixt them. The
navies on both fides were divided into three bat-

·tels. On the Englifh part, the earles of Glocester, Northampton, and Huntington, who was
admerall of the fleet that belonged to the cinque
ports, and the lorde Robert Morley, admerall of
the northerne navie, had the guiding of the fore
ward, bearing themfelves right valiantlie, fo that
at length the Englifhmen having the advantage,
not onlie of the funne, but alfo of the wind and
tide, fo fortunatlie, that the French fleet was
driven into the ftreights of the haven, in fuch
wife that neither the fouldiers nor mariners could
helpe themfelves, infomuch that both heaven, fea,
and wind, feemed all to have confpired againft
the Frenchmen. And herewith manie fhips of
Flanders joining themfelves with the Englifh fleet,
in the end the Frenchmen were vanquifhed, flaine
and taken, their fhips being alfo either taken,
bowged, or broken.

" When night was come upon them, there
were thirtie French fhips that yet had not entred
the battell, the which fought by covert of the
night to have ftolne awaie, and one of them being a mightie great vesfell, called the James of
Deepe, would have taken awaie a fhip of Sand-
wich that belonged to the prior of Canterburie: but
by the helpe of the erle of Huntington, after they
had fought all the night till the next morning,
the Englifhmen at length prevailed, and taking

that great huge fhip of Deepe, found in hir above foure hundred dead bodies. To conclude, verie few of the French fhips efcaped, except fome of their fmall vesfels, and certeine gallies with their admerall Barbe-noir, who in the beginning of the battell got foorth of the haven, advifing the other capteins to doo the like, thereby to avoide the danger which they wilfullie imbraced. There died in this battell, fought (as fome write) on midfummer-daie, in the yeare aforefaid, of French-men to the number of 30000, of Englifhmen about 4000, or (as other have that lived in thofe daies) not paft 400, amongft whom there were foure knights of great nobilitie, as fir Thomas Mon-hermere, fir Thomas Latimer, fir John Boteler, and fir Thomas Poinings.

" It faid alfo, that the king himfelfe was hurt in the thigh. The two Englifh fhips that had beene taken the yeere before, the Edward and the Christopher, were recovered at this time, amongft other of the French fhips that were taken there. Sir Peter Bahuchet was hanged upon a croffe pole faftened to a maft of one of the fhips *. Through the wilfulneffe of this man, the Frenchmen re-

* Fabian fays that both " fyr Nicholas Buchett" (as he calls him) "and fyr Hugh Querett, in defpite of the Frenche-men, were hanged upon the fayles of the fhippes, which they wer taken in."

ceived this loffe (as the French chronicles report)
bicaufe he kept the navie fo long within the haven, till they were fo inclofed by the Englifhmen,
that a great number of the Frenchmen could ne ·
ver come to ftrike ftroke, nor to ufe the fhot of
their artillerie, but to the hurt of their fellows.
Howfoever it was, the Englifhmen got a famous
victorie, to the great comfort of themfelves, and
difcomfort of their adverfaries. The king of England, after he had thus vanquifhed his enimies,
remained on the fea by the fpace of three daies,
and then comming on land, went to Gant, where
he wes received of the queene with great joy and
gladneffe." Holinfheds chronicle, 1587, vol. ii.
p. 358. See alfo Fabians, 1559. p. 211.

Page 19.

L. 14. —fir Robard out of Morlay.] Robert lord
Morley, admiral of the north navy of England ;
dyed in France, 1361.

L. 21. The erle of Norhamton.] William de Bo-
hun, created earl of Northampton in 1339; dyed
in 1359.

L. 23. Sir Walter the Mawnay.] Sir Walter
Manny, a native of Hainault, and the hero of a
romance in real life. See Froisfarts chronicle,
throughout. In performance of a promife he had
made " before ladyes and demofelles er he came
out of Englande," he " made the firft journey

into France," burnt a town, took a castle, and returned as if he had been taking a mornings ride.
Another time, in the courfe of an after-dinner converfation, in a befieged town, he propofes to isfue
out and break down a great engine ; which is in-
ftantly done, with equal gallantry and judgement.
King Edward and the prince of Wales fought under his banner at the battle of Calais.   He dyed,
full of glory and honour, in 1371, and was buryed in his own foundation of the Charter-houfe.

L. 25. *The duc of Lankaster.*] Henry (furnamed
de Grismond, otherwife *au tort col,* or wry neck)
then earl of Derby, who, fucceeding to the earl-
dom of Lancaster on the death of his father, in
1345, was, on the 6th of March 1351, created
duke of Lancaster.   He dyed in 1360, and was
buryed in the church of the college and hospital of
the New-works, at Leicester, which he had founded.   He was a brave and fortunate commander,
and makes a great figure in Froisfarts chronicle;
being at the fame time of a mild and generous dis-
pofition, and fo much beloved by the people as to
be ufually called *the good duke of Lancaster.*   His
piety, which may be now thought the leaft ad-
vantageous part of his character, procured him,
if not actual canonization, at leaft the title of
faint, a circumftance unnoticed by historians *.

* *"Testimonia ' Laurentii Divianenfis,' de præcipuis Car-
melitanæ religionis fautoribus, fcil. . . . .* SANCTO HENRICO

(92)

Page 20.

L. 3. *Sir Wiliam of Klinton.*] Sir William Clinton, created earl of Huntington in 1338, dyed in 1354.

L. 9. *The gude erle of Glowceter.*] Hugh Defpenfer; dyed in 1350.

Page 21.

L. 3. *The* Kogges of Ingland . . .] This feems the proper name of the fhip. The word *coggis* is ufed by bifhop Douglas in the fenfe of *boats* or *pinnaces:*

" And fum with airis into the *coggis* fmall
Ettilit to land."

The latter are now called *cocks* or *cock-boats.* The original word *cog* or *cogue* is ftill, in Scotland, the name of a wooden veffel ufed for fuping or drinking out of. *The Koggis of Ingland* is perhaps the identical fhip which Stow calls *the blacke Cocke.* In 1340, the earl of Gloucester, being to go to fea in the kings fervice, had two fhips asfigned to him out of the royal navy, *viz.*

PRIMO DUCE LANCASTRIÆ." MSS. Har. 1819. fo. 13. The houfe of Lancaster, indeed, was peculiarly diftinguifhed by *the odour of fanctity*; the miracles of his uncle, St. Thomas, were long celebrated; and that his defcendant, Henry VI. was not raifed to the fame honour, is folely afcribable to the avarice of his immediate fuccesfor of the fame name.

" the S. Mary *Cogg*, and the *Cogg* of Clyne.'"
(Dugdales *Baronage*, i. 395.) The *Cristofir* has
been already mentioned.

Page 22.

VI. HERKINS HOW KING EDWARD LAY
    WITH HIS MEN BIFOR TOURNAY.]
The king and his allies laid fiege to Tournay on
the   of July, 1340, and raifed it, by reafon
of a truce agreed upon between him and king
Philip, on the   of September in the fame year.
See Froisfarts chronicle, volume i. cc. 53, &c.

Page 24.

L. 13. *To ftop Philip the firate:*

    Ful ftill.] This fpecies of
verfe, which was probably common enough in
our authors time, though perhaps confined to
popular compofitions, now loft, is introduced,
for the fake of ridicule, no doubt, by Chaucer in
his *rime of fire Thopas.* Mr. Tyrwhitt, who had
not obferved the prefent inftance, nor met, it
feems, with any other, is very much at a lofs to
account for it. See his " Notes on *The Canterbury tales*" (iv. 37).

Page 24.

L. 18. *A duke tuke leve that tide.*] Froisfart af-
fords no ground to accufe the duke of treachery
or defection : he merely fays that, on raifing the

fiege, " the Brabances departed quickely, for they had 'great' defyre therto." Indeed it was faid that the befieged, whom the king thought to famifh, " founde fomme courtefy en theym of Brabaunt, in fufferynge vytayles to paſſe throughe their hooſt into the cytie: and they of Brusfels and Lovane were fore wery with taryeng there fo long, & they defyred the marſhall of thoſt that they might have leave to retourne into Brabant. The marſhall fayde, he was well content; but than they muſt leave all their harnes behynd them: with the which anſwere they were fo aſhamed that they never ſpake therof more." It is, however, highly probable that the duke, who was one of the king of Englands commisſioners to treat of the truce, might be particularly eager to have it concluded; fince the king " departed fore agaynſt his mynde, if he myght have done otherwyſe, but in maner he was fayne to folowe the wylles of the other lordes, and to byleve theyr counſayls."

Page 26.

L. 1. *Men may rede in romance right*

Of a grete clerk that Merlin *hight.*] Merlin, furnamed Ambrofius, the fon of an incubus, is a prophet and enchanter in the fabulous history or romance, profeſed to have been translated out of the ancient Britiſh language (but perhaps writen in original Latin) by Jeffrey of Monmouth, afterward bifhop of St. Afaph, about the year 1125. Vortegirn, king of the Britons, having been fpectator of a battle between two dragons, commands honeft Ambrofe to tell him what it portended: upon which he, burfting into tears, delivers, at fome length, the fuggeftions of his prophetical fpirit, in the courfe of which he fays: " From Conan fhall proceed a warlike boar, that fhall exercife the fharpnefs of his tufks within the Gallican woods. For he fhall cut down all the larger oaks, and fhall be a defence to the fmaller. The Arabians and Africans fhall dread him; for he fhall purfue his furious courfe to the farther part of Spain." See *The Britifh hiftory*, translated by Aaron Thompfon, 1718, p. 212. The author choofes to apply this image to his hero, whom he frequently, both in this and the following poems, calls *a bore* or *the bare*.

There was alfo another Merlin, furnamed *Silveftris*, or *Caledonius*, who prophefyed of king Charles II. under the figure of a boar. See *Britifh and outlandifh prophefies*, by Thomas Pugh, gentleman, 1658, 4to. p. 153.

Many copies of thefe prophecies, confiderably differing from each other, are ftill extant, both in French and Latin; but it would be a matter of difficulty, perhaps, to find the identical authority

vouched by our author *. It may, however, be
deemed fufficient for the prefent purpofe, to cite
the character of his hero from certain " Prophecies of Merlin," evidently compofed in their own
time, as extant in the Cotton MS.

" Efter the gayt † fall cum a lyon,
That in hert ful fers and fell fall be fun;
His bihalding fall be ful of petè,
His fembland to feke reft lykind fall be,
His breft alfwa fall be flokening of threft,
Untill all lufes pefe and reft,
His tong fall fpeke wordes all of lewtè,
His bering like a lamb meke fal be;
He fall have trey and tene in bigining,
To chistise misdoers of wrang lifing;
And als thurgh felnes fethin fall he feke,
Till he have made the folk als lamb to be meke.
He fall be cald in the werld, als wide als it es,
Bare of hele, of nobillay, and of felnes.
Als a lamb fall he [be] milde and meke,
And unto rightwisnes ay fall he feke.

* That part of Robert Mannyngs translation of Peter
Langtofts chronicle which contains the Britifh history has
not been publifhed; nor does the work exift in MS. elfewhere than in the Inner-Temple library. He may probably give the prophecy more in our authors manner.
† Edward II.

This ilk befte that es the bare named bifoṙn
Cumes out of Windefore, thare befe he born.
Whetand his tufkes fall that ilk baɾe
Fare thurgh foure landes thar he come never are;
And evermore his jornay ever ilka dele
Sall he do hardily, nobilly and wele;
Till the burgh of Jerufalem and to the haly land,
Sall he find none ogains him to ftand.
Spayne fall trembill for tene and for care,
Aragowne fall have drede and dout of the bare.
In France fall he fett his hevid biforn;
His tail fal reft in Yngland, whare he was born;
He fal whet his tufkes on Parifs zates;
Almayn fal be ful ferd for his lates.
He fall gar revers and mani grete flode
Be rinand with hernes and with rede blode.
The grefes that er grene fal he rede make;
Mani man for the bare fal trembill and quake.
In alkins landes win fall the bare
That any of his eldres has lofed are.
So nobil and fo doghty fall the bare be
That he fall or he dy were corons thre.
Underlout fall he mak ilk outen land
To be at his will and bow till his hand.
Wele more fall the bare conquer and win
Than ani did bifore of all his end kin.
All lordes fall him lout without ani lefe,
And than fall his land be in fwith gude pefeɩ

Sethin in a fer land end fall he,
And for his nobilles be graven bitwen kinges
thre."

Page 27.

L. 3. *For* John of France *will he noght spare.*]
John of France is John duke of Normandy, son
to king Philip, whom he succeeded on the 23d of
August, 1350.

L. 15. *For France now es he entred in.*] "Whan
the kynge of Englande," says Froissart, "ar-
ryved in the Hogue Saynt Waft*, the kinge ysfued out of his shyppe, and the fyrst fote that he
fette on the grounde, he fell so rudely that the
blode brafte out of his nofe: the knyghtes that
were aboute him toke him up, and fayd, Sir, for
goddes fake, enter in agayne into your shyp, and
come nat a lande this day; for this is but an evyll
fygne for us. Than the kyng answered quyckely
and fayd, Wherfore this is a good token for me,
for the lande desyreth to have me. Of the whiche
answere all his men were ryght joyful: so that day
and nyght the kynge lodged on the fandes, and
in the mean tyme dyscharged the shyppes of their
horfes and other bagages. There the kynge made
two marshals of his hooft, the one the lorde Godfray of Harecourt, and the other therle of Warwyke, and the erle of Arundell conftable. And

---

* La Hogue.

he ordayned that therle of Huntyngdon fhulde
kepe the flete of fhyppes with c. men of armes,
and foure c. archars. And alfo he ordeyned the
batayls, one to go on his ryght hande, clofynge to
the fee fyde, and the other on his lefte hande, and
the kynge himfelfe in the myddes, and every nyght
to lodge al in one felde. Thus they fette forth as
they were ordayned; and ... [after taking, rob-
ing, or burning the towns of " Harflewe, Cher-
bourgue, Mountbourgue, Quarentyne," and "many other townes in that country," and laftly, " a
great towne called Saynt Lowe,"] the kynge went
towarde Cane, the whiche was a greater towne,
and full of drapery, and other marchauntdyfe, and
ryche burgefses, noble ladyes and damofels, and
fayre churches, and fpecially two 'great' and
ryche abeys, one of the Trynytee, another of
faynt Stephyn ; and on the one fyde of the towne
one of the fayreft castells of all Normandy, and
capitayne therin was Roberte of Blargny, with
thre hundred Genowayes ; and in the towne was
therle of Ewe and of Guynes, conftable of Fraunce,
and therle of Tankervyll, with a good nombre of
men of warre. The king of England rode that
day in good order, and logedde al his batayls togyder that night, a two leages fro Cane, in a towne
with a lytell havyn called Haustreham ; and thyder came alfo all his navy of fhyppes, with therle of

Huntyngdone, who was governour of them. The conftable and other lordes of France that nyght watched well the towne of Cane, and in the morn-ynge armed them, with all them of the towne. Than the conftable ordayned that none fhulde ys-fue out, but kepe their defences on the walles, gate, bridge, and ryver, and lette the fubbarbes voyde, bycaufe they were nat clofedde, for they thought they fhulde have ynough to do to defende the towne, bycaufe it was nat clofedde but with the ryver. They of the towne fayde howe they wolde ysfue out, for they were ftronge ynough to fyght with the kyng of Englande. Whan the conftable fawe their goodwyls, he fayde, In the name of god, be it; ye fhall not fyght without me. Than they ysfued oute in good order; and made good face to fyght, and to defende theym, and to putte their lyves in adventure.

" The fame daye thenglyfh men rofe erly, and appayrelled them redy to go to Cane : the kynge harde noyfe before the fonne-ryfinge; and than toke his horfe, and the prince his fon, with fir Godfraye of Harcourt, marfhall and leader of all the hooft, whofe counfayle the kynge moche fo-lowed. Than they drewe towarde Cane with their batels in good aray; and fo aproched the good towne of Cane. Whanne they of the towne, who were redy in the felde, fawe thefe thre batayls

commyng in good order, with their baners and
ftanderdes wavynge in the wynde, and the archers,
the which they had nat bene accustomed to fe,
they were fore afrayd, and fledde away towarde
the towne, without any order or good aray, for
all that the conftable coulde do: than the Englyfhmen purfued them egerly. Whan the conftable, and the erle of Tankervyll fawe that, they
toke a gate at the entry, and faved themfelf and
certayne with them; for the Englyfhmen were
entred into the towne. Some of the knyghtes and
fquyers of Fraunce, fuche as knewe the waye to
the castell, went thyder, and the captayne there received them all, for the castell was large. Thenglyfhmen in the chafe flewe many, for they toke
none to mercy. Than the conftable and the erle
of Tankervyll, beynge in the lytell towre at the
bridge fote, loked alonge the ftrete, and faw their
men flayne without mercy, they douted to fall
in their handes. At laft they fawe an Englyffhe
knyght with one eye, called fir Thomas Holande,
and a fyve or fixe other knyghtes with hym; they
knewe them, for they had fene them before in
Pruce, in Grenade, and other vyages: than they
called to fir Thomas, and fayde howe they wolde
yelde themfelfe prifoners. Than fir Thomas came
thider with his company, and mounted up into
the gate, and there founde the fayde lordes with

xxv. knyghtes with them, who yelded them to fir Thomas, and he toke them for his prifoners, and left company to kepe theym; and than mounted agayne on his horfe, and rode into the ftreates, and faved many lyves, of ladyes, damofels, and cloysterers fro defoylynge, for the foudyers were without mercy. It fell fo well the fame feafon for thenglyffhmen, that the ryver, whiche was able to bere fhyppes at that tyme, was fo lowe that men went in and out befyde the bridge. They of the towne were entred into their houfes, and caft downe into the ftrete ftones, tymbre and yron; and flewe and hurte mo than' fyve hundred En - glyffhmen, wherwith the kynge was fore displeafed. At nyght whan he hard therof, he commaunded that the next daye all fhulde be putte to the fwerde and the towne brent; but than fir Godfray of Harecourt fayd: Dere fir, for goddes fake, asfwage fomewhat youre courage; and let it fuffyce you that ye have done. Ye have yet a great voyage to do, er ye come before Calys, whyder ye purpofe to go; and, fir, in this towne there is moche people, who wyll defend their houfes; and it woll coft many of your men their lyves, er ye have all at your wyll; wherby, paraventure, ye fhall nat kepe your purpofe to Calys, the whiche fhulde redowne to your rech. Sir, fave your people; for ye fhall have nede of them or this moneth paffe;

for i thynke verely your adverfary kynge Philyppe
woll mete with you to fyght, and ye fhall fynde
many ftrayt pasfages and rencounters. Wherfore
your men, and ye had mo, fhall ftande you in
gode ftede: and, fir, without any further fleynge,
ye fhall be lorde of this towne, men and women
woll put 'al' that they have to your pleafure.
Than the kyng fayd, Sir Godfraye, you ar our
marfhall; ordayne every thynge as ye woll. Than
fir Godfray, with his baner, rode fro ftrete to
ftrete, and commaunded in the kynges name, non
be fo hardy to put fyre in any houfe, to flee any
perfone, nor to vyolate any woman. Whan they
of the towne hard that crye, they receyved the
Englyfhmen into their houfes, and made theym
good chere; and fome opyned their coffers, an
badde them take what them lyft, fo they myght
be asfured of ther lyves: howe beit there were
done in the towne many yvell dedes, 'murders'
and roberyes. Thus the Englyfhmen were lordes
of the towne thre dayes, and wanne great richeffe,
the which they fent by barkeffe and barges to
Saynte Savyoure, by the ryver of Austreben a
two leages thens; where as all their navy lay.
Than the kyng . . . departed fro the towne of
Cane, and rode in the fame maner as he dyde before; brennynge and exilynge the countrey."
(Vol. i. cc. 122, &c.)

Page 28.

L. 24. *The toun of* Cane *thai fet on fire.*] This
is a mistake, as appears from the precedeing ex-
tract. After leaving Caen, the king burnt the
town of " Gyfors, Saynte Germayne in Laye,
Mountjoy, Saynte Clowde, Petit Bolayne by Pa-
rys, and the quenes Bourge." On quiting the
vicinity of Paris he hanged twenty of his men for
feting fire to the fair and rich abbey of Saint
Mesfine near to Beauvais, the fuburbs of which
town were burnt, as was alfo the town of Poys.
See Froisfart, vol. i. c. 125.

Page 29.

L. 10. *At* Creffy *when thai* brak the brig.] No
particular mention is made by Froisfart of the
breaking of this bridge; he only fays that " the
kyng of Englande being at Araynes wyft nat
where for to paffe the Some, the which was large
and depe, and all briges were brokin, and the
pasfages well kept."

L. 14. *Over that water er thai went.*] " Whan
' the Frenche kyng' was at Amyenfe he had ordayned a great barowne of Normandy, called fir
Godmar du Fay, to go and kepe the pasfade of
Blanche Taque, where the Englyffhmen muft
paffe, or els in none other place: he had with
hym m. men of armes, and fixe thoufand a fote,
with the Genowayes; foo they went by Saynte

Reyngnyer in Ponthieu, and fro thens to Crotay,
whereas the pasfage lay. And alfo he had with
hym a great nombre of men of the countrey, and
alfo a great nombre of theym of Mutterell; fo
that they were a twelfe thoufand men, one and
other. Whan the Englyflhe hooft was come thyder, fir Godmar du Fay araunged all his company
to defende the pasfage. The kyng of Englande
lette nat for all that, but whanne the fludde was
gone, he commaunded his marfhall to entre into
the water, in the name of god and faynt George.
Than they that were hardy and coragyous entred
in bothe parties, and many a man reverfed: there
were fome of the Frenchmen of Arthoyes and
Pycardy that were as gladde to juft in the water
as on the drye lande. The Frenchemen defended
fo well the pasfage at the ysfuyng out of the water, that they had moche to do: the Genowayes
dyde them great trouble with their crosbowes.
On thother fyde the archers of Englande fhotte fo
holly togyder, that the Frenchmen were fayne to
gyve place to the Englyflhmen. There was a fore
batayle, and many a noble feate of armes done on
both parties: finally thenglyflhmen pafsed over,
and asfembled togyder in the felde. The kynge
and the prince pafsed, and all the lordes: than the
Frenchmen kept none array, but departed he that
might beft. Whan fir Godmar fawe that discon-

fyture, he fledde and faved hymfelfe: fome fledde
to Abvyle, and fome to Saynte Raygnyer. They
that were there a fote coude nat flee, fo that there
were flayne a great numbre of them of Abvyle,
Muttrell, Arras, and of Saynt Reygnier: the
chafe endured more than a great leag. And as
yet all the Englyfhmen were nat pafsed the ryver, certayne currours of the kyng of Behayne,
and of fir Johan of Heynaultes, came on them
that were behind, and toke certayne horfes and
caryages, and flewe dyvers, or they coude take
the pasfage." Froisfart, vol. i. c. 127.

L. 21. *He faw the toun o ferrum bren.*] Our
author is ftill fpeaking, it would feem, of the town
of Cane; for, if he means the town of Cresfy, he
muft have been misinformed, as Crotay feems to
have been the only place burnt after the king
paffed the river. He arrived on Friday the 14th
of Auguft, 1346, in the neighbourhood of Cresfy, where he encamped: the king of France lying
with a great army at Abbeville.

Page 30.

L. 1. *Than come Philip ful redy dight,* &c.] This
is the famous battle of Cresfy, of which Froisfarts
account, though fomewhat prolix, is very curious
and minute. " On the Fridaye, as i fayde before, the kyng of Englande lay in the feldes; for
the contrey was plentyfull of wynes and other vy-

tayle; and yf nede had bene they had provyfyon
folowynge in cartes and other caryages. That
nyght the kynge mad a fupper to all his chefe
lordes of the hooft, & made them good chere:
and whan they were all departed to take their
reft, than the kynge entred into his oratorie, and
kneled downe before the auter, praeng god de-
voutly, that if he fought the next day that he
might achyve the journey to his honour. Than
aboute midnyght he layde hym downe to refte;
and in the mornynge he rofe betymes, and harde
maffe, and the prince his fonne with hym; and
the mofte parte of his company were confefsed and
houfeled: and, 'after' the maffe fayde, he commaunded every man to be armed, & to drawe to
the felde, to the fame place before apoynted. Than
the kynge caufed a parke to be made by the wode
fyde, behynde his hooft; and there was fet all
cartes and caryages, and within the parke were
all their horfes, for every man was afote: and
into thys parke there was but one entry. Than
he ordayned thre batayls. In the firft, the yonge
prince of Wales, with hym the erle of Warwyke
and Canforde, the lorde Godfray of Harecourt,
fir Reynolde Cobham, fir Thomas Holande, the
lorde Stafforde, the lorde of Mauny, the lorde
Dalaware, fir Johan Chandos, fir Bartylmewe de
Bomes, fir Roberte Nevyll, the lorde Thomas

Clyfforde, the lorde Bourchier, the lorde de la
Tumyer, and dyvers other knytes and fquyers
that i can nat name: they were an viii. hundred
men of armes, and two thoufande archers, and a
thoufande of other, with the Walffhmen : every
lorde drue to the felde apoynted, under his owne
baner and penone. In the fecond batayle, was
therle of Northampton, the erle of Arundell, the
lorde Roffe, the lorde Lygo, the lorde Wylough-
by, the lorde Basfet, the lorde of Saynt Aubyne,
fir Loyes Tueton, the lorde of Myleton, the lorde
de la Sell, and dyvers other, about an eight hundred men of armes, and twelf hundred archers.
The third batayle had the kynge: he had fevyn
hundred men of armes and two thoufande archers. Than the kyng lept on a hobby, with a
whyte rodde in his hand, one of his marfhals on
the one hande, and the other on the other hande :
he rode fro renke to renke, defyringe every man
to take hede that daye to his right and honour.
He fpake it fo fwetely, and with fo good countenance and mery chere, that all fuch as were disconfyted toke courage in the fayeng and heryng
of hym. And whan he had thus vifyted all his ba-
tayles, it was then nyne of the day : than he caufed
every man to eate & drynke a lytell, and fo they
dyde at their leafer ; and afterwarde they ordred
agayne their bataylles : than every man lay downe

on the yerthe, and by hym his falet and bowe, to
be the more freſſher whan their ennemyes ſhulde
come.

" This Saturdaye the Frenche kynge roſe betymes, and hard maſſe in Abvyle, in his lodgynge
in the abey of Saynte Peter; and he departed after the ſonne-riſyng. Whan he was out of the
towne two leages, aprochyng towarde his ennemyes, ſome of his lordes ſayde to hym: Sir, it
were good that ye ordred your batayls, and let
all your fotemen paſſe ſomwhat on before, that
they be nat troubled with the horſemen. Than
the kyng ſent iiii. knyghtes, the Moyne Battell,
the lorde of Noyers, the lorde of Beaujewe, and
the lorde Dambegny, to ryde to avyewe theng-
lyſſhe hoſte: and ſo they rode ſo nere that they
myght well ſe part of their dealyng. Thenglyſſhmen ſawe them well, and knewe well howe they
were come thyder to avieu them: they let them
alone, and made no countenance towarde them,
and let them retourne as they came. And whan
the Frenche kyng ſawe theſe foure knyghtes
retourne agayne, he taryed tyll they came to
hym; and ſayd, Sirs, what tydynges? Theſe four
knyghtes eche of them loked on other, for there
was none wolde ſpeke before his companyon.
Finally, the kynge ſayd to Moyne, who pertayned
to the kynge of Behaygne, and had done in his

dayes fomoch that he was reputed for one of the valyanteft knightes of the worlde, Sir, fpeke you. Than he fayd: Sir, I fhall fpeke, fith it pleafeth you, under the correction of my felawes: fir, we have ryden and fene the behavynge of your ennemyes, knowe ye for trouth, they are refted in thre batayls, abydinge for you. Sir, I woll counfell you, as for my parte, favynge your displeafure, that you and all your company reft here and lodg for this nyght; for or they that be behynde of your company be come hyther, and or your batayls be fet in good order, it wyll be very late, and your people be wery and out of array; and ye fhall fynde your ennemys freffhe and redy to receyve you. Erly in the mornynge ye maye order your bataylles at more leafer, and advife your ennemies at more delyberacion, and to regarde well what way ye wyll asfayle theym; for, fir, furely they woll abyde you. Than the kynge commaunded that it fhuld be fo done. Than his ii. marfhals one rode before, another behynde, fayenge to every baner, Tary and abyde here, in the name of god and faynt Denys. They that were formaft taryed; but they that were behynde wolde nat tary, but rode forthe, and fayd howe they wold in no wyfe abyde tyll they were as ferre forward as the formaft. And whan they before fawe them come on behynde, than they rode for-

warde agayne; fo that the kyng nor his marfhals
coude nat rule them. So they rode withoute order in good araye, tyll they came in fyght of their
enemyes. And asfone as the formaft fawe them,
they reculed than backe without good araye,
wherof they behynde had marvell, and were abafh-
ed, and thought that the formaft compani had
ben fightyng: than they myght have had leafer
and rome to have gone forwarde if they had lyft.
Some went forthe, and fome abode ftyll. The
commons, of whome all the wayes bytwene Abvyle and Cresfy were full, whan they fawe that
they were nere to their ennemies, they toke their
fwerdes, and cryed, Downe with them, let us fle
them all. There was no man, though he were
prefent at the journey, that coude ymagen or fhewe
the trouth of the yvell order that was amonge the
Frenche partie; and yet they were a mervelous
greate nombre. That i wryte in this boke, i lern-
ed it fpecyally of the Englyfhmen, who well behelde their dealyng; and alfo certayne knyghtes of
fir Johan of Henaultes, who was alwayes aboute
kynge Philyppe, fhewed me as they knewe.

" Thenglyfhmen, who were in thre batayls
lyenge on the grounde to reft them, asfone as they
faw the Frenchmen aproche, they rofe upon their
fete, fayre and eafely, withoute any haft, and
aranged their batayls. The firfte, whiche was

the princes batell, the archers there ſtode in maner of a herſe, and the men of armes, in the bo-
tome of the batayle. Therle of Northamton &
therle of Arundell, with the ſecond batell, were
on a wynge in good order, redy to confute the
princes batayle, yf nede were. The lordes and
knyghtes of France came nat to the asſemble togyder in good order; for ſome came before, and
ſome came after, in ſuche haſt and yvell order,
that one of them dyd trouble another. Whan the
French kyng ſawe the Englyſſhmen, his blode
chaunged, and ſayde to his marſhals, Make the
Genowayes go on before, and begynne the batayle,
in the name of god and ſaynt Denyſe. There
were of the Genowaies, crosbowes, about a fyftene thouſand, but they were ſo wery of goyng
a fote that day a ſix leages, armed with their crosbowes, that they ſayde to their conſtables, We be
nat well ordred to fyght this daye, for we be nat
in the caſe to do any great dede of armes; we
have more nede of reſt. Theſe wordes came to
the erle of Alanſon, who ſayd, A man is well at
eaſe to be charged with ſuche a ſorte of rascalles,
to be faynt and fayle nowe at mooſt nede! Alſo,
the ſame ſeaſon, there fell a greate rayne and a
clyps, with a terryble thonder; and before the
rayne there came fleyng over bothe batayls a great
nombre of crowes, for feare of the tempeſt com-

myng. Than anone the eyre beganne to waxe clere, and the fonne to fhyne fayre and bright; the whiche was right in the Frenchmens eyen, and on the Englyffhmens backe. Whan the Genowayes were asfembled toguyder, and beganne to aproche, they made a great leape and crye to abaffhe thenglyffhmen; but they ftode ftyll, and ftyredde nat for all that. Thanne the Genowayes, agayne the feconde tyme, made another leape and a fell crye, and ftepped forwarde a lytell; and thenglyffhmen remeved nat one fote. Thirdly, agayne they leapt and cryed, and went forthe tyll they came within fhotte: thanne they fhotte ficrsly with their crosbowes. Than thenglyffhe archers ftepte furthe one pafe, and lette fly their arowes, fo holly and fo thycke, that it femed fnowe. Whan the Genowayes felte the arowes perfynge through ' heeds,' armes, and breftes, many of them caft downe their crosbowes, and dyde cutte their ftrynges, and retourned disconfyted. Whan the Frenche kynge fawe them flye awaye, he fayde, Slee thefe rafcals, for they fhall lette and trouble us withoute reafon. Than ye fhulde have fene the men of armes daffhe in among them, and kylled a great nombre of them. And ever ftyll the Englyflimen fhot where as they fawe thyckeft preace: the fharpe arowes ranne into the men of armes, and into their horfes, and

I

many fell, horfe and men, amonge the Genoweys;
and whan they were downe, they coude nat re-
lyve agayne, the preace was fo thycke, that one
overthrewe another. And alfo amonge the Englyffhmen there were certayne rascalles, that went
afote, with greate knyves; and they went in
among the men of armes, and flewe and mur-
dredde many, as they laye on the grounde; bothe
erles, ' barownes,' knyghtes, and fquyers : wherof the kyng of Englande was after difpleafed ; for
he had rather they had bene taken prifoners. The
valyant kynge of Behaygne, called Charles of Luzenbourge, fonne to the noble emperour Henry
of Luzenbourge, for all that he was nyghe blynde,
whan he underftode the order of the batayle, he
fayde to them about hym, Where is the lorde
Charles my fon ? His men fayde, Sir, we cannat
tell; we thynke he be fyghtynge. Than he fayde,
Sirs, ye are my men, my companyons, and frendes,
in this journey ; i requyre you bryng me fo farre
forwarde, that i maye ftryke one ftroke with my
fwerde. They fayde they wolde do his com-
maundemente; and to the entent that they fhulde
nat lefe hym in the preafe, they tyed all their
raynes of their bridelles eche to other, and fette
the kynge before to acomplyffhe his defyre; and
fo they went on their enemyes. The lorde Charles
of Behaygne, his fonne, who wrote hymfelfe kynge

of Behaygne, and bare the armes, he came in
good order to the batayle, but whanne he fawe
that the matter wente awrye on their parte, he
departed, i can nat tell you whiche waye. The
kynge his father was fo farre forewarde, that he
ftrake a ftroke with his fwerde, ye and mo than
fought valyantly; and fo dyde his company, and
they adventured themfelfe fo forwarde that they
were all flayne, and the next day they were founde
in a place about the kynge, and all the horfes tyed
eche to other . . . This batayle bytwene Broy and
Crefly, this Saturday, was ryght cruell and fell,
and many a feat of armes done that came not to
my knowlege. In the night dyverfe knyghtes
and fquyers loft their maisters, and fomtyme came
on thenglyffhmen, who receyved theym in fuche
wyfe, that they were ever nighe flayne; for there
was none taken to mercy nor to raunfome; for fo
the Englyffhmen were determyned in the mornyng
[of] the day of the batayle. Certayne Frenchemen and Almaygnes perforce opyned the archers
of the princes batayle, and came and fought with
the men of armes hande to hande. Than the feconde batayle of thenglyffhmen came to focour the
princes batayle; the whiche was tyme, for they
had as than moche ado; and they with the prince
fent a mesfenger to the kynge, who was on a lytell wyndmyll hyll. Than the knyght fayde to

the kynge, Sir, therle of Warwyke, and therle of
Canfort, fir Reynolde Cobham, and other fuche
• as be about the prince your fonne, ar feersly
fought withall, and are fore handled : wherfore
they defyre you that you and your batayle wolle
come and ayde them, for if the Frenchmen encreafe,
as they dout they woll, your fonne and they fhall
have moche ado. Than the kynge fayde, Is my
fonne deed, or hurt, or on the yerthe felled ? No,
fir, quoth the knyght, but he is hardely matched ;
wherfore he hathe nede of your ayde. Well, fayde
the kyng, retourne to hym, and to them that fent
you hyther, and fay to them, that they fende no
more to me for any adventure that falleth, as long
as my fonne is alyve : and alfo fay to them, that
they fuffre hym this day to wynne his fpurres ;
for, if god be pleafed, i woll this journey be his,
and the honoure therof, and to them that be
aboute hym. Than the knyght retourned agayn
to them, and fhewed the kynges wordes, the which
gretly encouraged them ; and repoyned in that
they had fende to the kynge as they dyd . . . .
In the evenynge the Frenche kynge, who had left
about hym no mo than a threefcore perfons one
and another, wherof fir Johan of Heynalt was
one, who had remounted ons the kynge, for his
horfe was flayne with an arowe ; than he fayde to
the kynge, Sir, departe henfe, for it is tyme : lefe

nat yourfelfe wylfully: if ye have loffe at this
tyme, ye fhall recover it agayne another feafon.
And foo he toke the kinges horfe by the brydell,
and ledde hym away in a maner perforce . . . .
This Saturday the Englyffhemen never departed
fro their batayls for chafynge of any man, but
kept ftyll their felde, and ever defended themfelfe
agaynft all fuch as came to asfayle them. This
batayle ended aboute evynfonge tyme.

"On this Saturdaye, whan the nyght was come,
and that thenglyffhmen hard no more noyfe of
the Frenchemen, than they reputed themfelfe to
have the vyctorie, and the Frenchmen to be dys-
confited, flayne and fled awaye. Than they made
greate fyers, and lyghted up torcheffe and can-
delles, bycaufe it was very darke; than the kyng
avayled downe fro the lytell hyll whereas he ftode,
and of al that day tyll than his helme came never
of on his heed. Than he went with all his batayle
to his fonne the prince, and fayde, Fayre fonne,
god gyve you good perfeverance; ye ar my good
fon, thus ye have acquyted you nobly; ye ar worthy to kepe a realme. The prince inclyned himfelfe to the yerthe, honouryng the kyng his father. This night they thanked god for their
good adventure, and made no booft therof; for
the kynge wolde that no manne fhulde be proude
or make booft, but every man humbly to thank

god." Froisſarts chronicle, vol. i. cc. 128, 129, 130, 131.

Page 34.

VII. How EDWARD, ALS THE ROMANCE SAIS, HELD THE SEGE BIFOR CALAYS.]

" Whan the kyng of Englande was come before Calys *, he layde his ſiege and ordayned bastides, betwene the towne and the ryver; he made carpenters to make houſes, and lodgynges of great tymbre, and ſet the houſes lyke ' ſtreetes,' and coverd them with rede and brome; ſo that it was lyke a lytell towne; and there was every thynge to ſell, and a markette-place to be kept every Tueſdaye and Saturday, for fleſſhe and fyſſh, mercery-ware, houſes for cloth, for bredde, wyne and all other thynges necesſarie, ſuche as came out of England, or out of Flanders, there they myght bye what they lyſt . . . The kynge wolde nat asfayle the towne of Calys; for he thought it but a loſt labour : he ſpared his peple, & his artillery, and ſayd howe he wold famyſſhe them in the towne with long ſiege, without the Frenche kyng come and reyſe his ſiege perforce. Whan the capten of Calys ſawe the maner and thorder of thenglyſſhmen, than he conſtrayned all poore aud meane peple to ysſue out of the towne. And on

* On the 3d of September, 1346.

Wednyſday there ysſued out, of men, women and
chyldren, mo than xvii.c. and as they paſsed
through the hooſt, they were demaunded why
they departed, and they anſwered and ſayde, bycauſe they had nothyng to lyve on. Than the
kyng dyd them that grace that he ſuffred them
to paſſe through his hoſt without danger, and
gave them mete and drynke to dyner, and every
perſon , ii.d. ſterlyng in almes; for the which dy-
ners many of them prayed for the kynges proſpe-
ryte.

"Kinge Philyppe, who knewe well howe his
men were ſore conſtrayned in Calays, commaunded every manne to be with hym at the feeſt of
Pentecoſt, in the citie of Amyenſe, or there about:
there was none durſt ſay nay . . . Whan they were
all at Amyenſe they toke counſayle; the Frenche
kyng wold gladly that the paſſages of Flaunders
myght have ben opyned to hym: for than he
thought he might ſende part of his men to Gra-
velyng, and by that way to refreſſhe the towne
of Calys, and on that ſyde to fyght eaſely with
thenglyſſhmen. He ſende great meſſangers into
'Flaunders' to treat for that mater, but the kyng
of Englande had there ſuche frendes that they
wolde never accorde to that curteſy: than the
Frenche kyng ſaid howe he wolde go thyder on
the ſyde towarde Burgoyne . . . . Than the kyng

went to the towne of Arras, and fette many men
of warre to the garyfons of Arthoys . . . Than
the French kyng and his company departed fro
Arras and went to Hedyn; his hooft with the ca-
ryage held well in length a three leages of that
contrey ; and there he taryed a day, and the next
day to Blangy. There he refted to take advyfe
what way to go forthe : than he was counfayled
to go through the contrey called la Belme, and
that way he toke, and with him a cc.m. one and
other ; and fo . . . came ftreyght to the byll of
Sangattes, bytwene Calays and Wysfant. They
came in goodly order with baners displayed, that
hit was great beautie to beholde their puysfant
array : they of Calys, whan they fawe them lodge,
it femed to them a newe fiege.

" Ye fhall here what the kyng of Englande
dyd . . . Whanne he fawe and knewe that the
Frenche kyng came with fo great an hooft to rayfe
the fiege, the whiche had cofte him fo moche good,
and payne of his body, and loft many of hys men,
and knewe well howe he had fo conftrayned the
towne, that hit coulde nat longe endure for de-
faute of vitayls, it greved hym fore than to depart. Than he advyfed well howe the Frenchmen coude nat aproche nother to the hooft, nor
to the towne, but in two places, other by the
downes by the fee fyde, or elles above by the

highe waye, and there was many dykes, rockes,
and mareſſhes, and but one way to paſſe over the
bridge called Newlande bridge. Than the kynge
made all his navy to drawe along by the coſt of
the downes, every ſhyp well garnyſſhed with bom-
bardes, crosbowes, archers, ſpringalles, and other
artyllary; wherby the Frenche hooſt myght nat
paſſe that waye. And the kyng cauſed the erle
of Derby to go and kepe Newlande-bridge with a
great nombre of men of armes and archers, ſo
that the Frenchmen coude natte paſſe no waye,
'without' they wolde have gone through the
marſhes, the whiche was unposſyble. On the
other ſyde, towarde Calays, there was a hygh
towre kept with xxx. archers, and they kept the
pasſages of the downes fro the Frenchmen . . .
The Frenche kyng ſent his marſhals to advyſe
what way he myght aproche to fyght with the
Englyſſhmen : ſo they went forthe, and whan
'they' had advyſed the pasſages and ſtraytes,
they retourned to the kyng, and ſayde, howe in
no wyſe he coude come to the Englyſſhmen, without he wolde leſe his people. So the mater reſted
all that day and nyght after. The next day, after maſſe, the Frenche kynge ſende to the kynge
of Englande the lord ' Geffraye' of Charney, the
lord Ewſtace of Rybamount *, Guy of Nele,

* This nobleman was taken priſoner, in ſingle combat,
by king Edward, fighting under the banner of ſir Walter

and the lorde Beajewe; and as they rode that ftronge waye, they fawe well it was harde to paffe that way. They prayfed moche the order that the erle of Derby kept there at the bridge of New-lande, by the whiche they pafsed. Than they rode tyll they came to the kynge, who was well acompanyed with noble men aboute hym; thanne they foure lyghted, and came to the kynge, and dyde their reverence to hym. Than the lord Ewftace of Rybamount faid, Sir, the kynge my mayster fendeth you worde by us that he is come to the mount of Sangate to do batayle with you; but he canne fynde no way to come to you: ther-fore, fir, he wolde that ye fhulde apoynt certayne of your counfayle, and in lyke wife of his, and they betwene theym to advyfe a place for the ba-tayle. The kyng of Englande was redy advyfed to anfwere, and fayde, Sirs, I have well underftande that ye defyre me, on the behalfe of myne adver-fary, who kepeth wrongfully fro me myne hery-tage: wherfore i am forie. Say unto hym fro me, if ye lyft, that i am here, and fo have bene nyghe an hole yere, and all this he knew right well. He

Manny, at the battle of Calais, in 1349. The night after the battle the king gave his prifoners a fupper in the castle of Calais, and after fupper, he gave fir Euftace a chaplet of pearls from his own head, as the moft valiant knight of the world, and fet him free without ranfom. See Froisfart, v. I. cc. 151, 152.

myght have come hyther foner, if he had wolde;
but he hath fuffred me to abide here fo long, the
whiche hath ben gretly to my cofte and charge.
I nowe coude do fo moche, if i wolde, to be fone
lorde of Calays, wherfore I am natte determynedde
to folowe his devyfe and eafe, nor to departe fro
that whiche i am at the poynt to wynne, and that
i have fo fore defyred, and derely 'boughte:' wherfore if he nor his men canne paffe this way, lette
theym feke fome other pasfage, if they thynke to
come hyther. Thanne thefe lordes departed, and
were conveyed tyll they were pafte Newlande
bridge: than they fhewed the Frenche kynge the
kynge of Englandes anfwere.

" In the meane feafone, whyle the Frenche
kynge ftudyed howe to fight with the kyng of
Englande, there came into his hooft two cardynalles from biffhoppe Clement in legacion, who
toke great payne to ryde bytwene thefe hooftes;
and they procuredde fo moche that ther was
graunted a certayne treatie of acorde, and a re-
fpyte bytwene the two kynges, and ther men,
beynge there at fiege and in the felde all onely.
And fo there were four lordes apoynted on ey-
ther partie to counfell togyder, and to treat for
peace . . . and the two cardynalles were meanes
betwene the parties. ' Thefe' lordes mette thre
dayes, and many devyfes put forthe, but none

effecte . . . than the two cardynalles returned to
Saynt-Omers; and whan the Frenche kynge fawe
that he coude do nothynge, the next daye he dys-
loged by tymes, and toke his way to 'Amyens,'
and gave every man leve to depart.

" After that the Frenche kynge was thus departed fro Sangate, they within Calays fawe well
howe their focoure fayled them; for the whiche
they were in great forowe. Than they defyred
fo moche their captayn, fir Johan of Vyen, that
he went to the walles of the towne, and made a
fygne to fpeke with fome perfon of the hooft.
Whan the kynge harde therof, he fende thyder
fir Galtier of Manny, and fir Basfet. Than fir
Johan of Vyen fayd to them : Sirs, ye be ryght
valyant knyghtes in dedes of armes; and ye knowe
well howe the kynge my mayster hath fende me
and other to this towne, and commaunded us to
kepe it to his behofe, in fuche wyfe that we take
no blame, nor to hym no dammage; and we have
done all that lyeth in oure power. Now oure fo-
cours hath fayled us; and we be fo fore ftrayned,
that we have nat to lyve withall, but that we
mufte all dye, or els enrage for famyn; without
the noble and gentyll kyng of yours woll take
mercy on us, the whiche to do we requyre you to
defyre hym to have pyte on us, and to let us go
and depart as we be; and lette hym take the

towne and castell, and all the goodes that be therin, the whiche is greate abundaunce. Than ſir
Gaultyer of Manny ſayde, Sir, we knowe ſomwhat of the entencyon of the kynge our mayster,
for he hath ſhewed it unto us: ſurely, knowe, for
trouth, it is nat his mynde that ye, nor they
within the towne, ſhulde depart ſo; for it is his
wyll that ye all ſhude put yourſelfes into his pure
wyll, to ranſome all ſuche as pleaſeth hym, and
to putte to dethe ſuche as he lyſte: for they of
Calays hath done hym ſuche contraryes and dis-
pyghtes, and hath cauſed hym to dyſpende ſoo
moche good, and loſte many of his menne, that
he is ſore greved agaynſt them. Than the captayne ſayde, Sir, this is to harde a mater to us;
we ar here within a ſmall forte of knightes and
ſquyers, who hath trewely ſerved the kyng our
maiſter, as well as ye ſerve yours. In lyke caſe,
and we have endured moche payne and uneaſe,
but we ſhall yet endure asmoche payne as ever
knyghtes dyd, rather thanne to conſent that the
worſt ladde in the towne ſhulde have any more
yvell than the greteſt of us all. Therfore, ſir, we
praye you, that of your humylite, yet that ye
woll go and ſpeke to the kynge of Englande; and
deſyre hym to have pitie of us; for we truſte in
hym ſo moche gentylneſſe, that by the grace of
god, his purpoſe ſhall chaunge. Sir Galtier of

Manny and fir Basfet retourned to the kynge, and declared to hym all that hadde bene fayde. The kynge fayde, he wolde none other wyfe, but that they fhulde yelde them up fymply to his pleafure. Than fir Gaultier fayde, Sir, favynge your dis-pleafure in this, ye may be in the wronge; for ye fhall gyve by this an yvell enfample. If ye fende any of us your fervauntes into any fortreffe, we woll nat be very gladde to go, if ye putte any of theym in the town to dethe after they be yelded: for in lyke wife they woll deale with us, if the cafe fell lyke. The whiche wordes dyverfe other lordes that were there prefent fustayned and mayn-teyned. Than the kynge fayde, Sirs, i wyll nat be alone agaynfte you all; therfore, fir Gaultier of Many, ye fhall goo, and faye to the captayne, that all the grace that they fhall fynde nowe in me is, that they lette fixe of the chief burgefses of the towne 'come' out bareheeded, barefoted and barelegged, and in their fhertes, with haulters about their neckes, with the kayes of the towne and castell in their handes; and lette theym fixe yelde themfelfe purely to my wyll, and the refy-dewe i wyll take to mercy. Than fyr Gaultyer retourned, and founde fyr Johan of Vyen ftyll on the wall, abydynge for an anfwere: thanne fir Gaultyer fhewed hym all the grace that he coulde gette of the kynge. Well, quod fir Johan, fir, i

requyre you tary here a certayne fpace, tyll i go
in to the towne, and fhewe this to the commons
of the towne, who fent me hyder. Than fir Johan
went unto the market-place, and founed the common bell; than incontynent men and women asfembled there: than the captayne made reporte
of all that he had done, and fayde, Sirs, it wyll
be none otherwyfe; therfore nowe take advyfe,
and make a fhorte aunfwere. Thanne all the people beganne to wepe, and to make fuche forowe,
that there was nat fo herd a hert, yf they had fene
them, but that wolde have had greate pytie cn
theym: the captayne hymfelfe wepte pytiously.
At laft the mooft ryche burgeffe of all the towne,
called Ewftace of Saynte-Peters, rofe up and fayde
openly: Sirs, great and fmall, greate myschiefe it
fhulde be to fuffre to dye fuche people as be in
this towne, other by famyn or otherwyfe, whan
there is meane to fave theym. I thynke he or
they fhulde have great merette of our lorde god,
that myght kepe theym fro fuche myscheife. As
for my parte, i have fo good trufte in our lorde
god, that yf i dye in the quarell to fave the refy-
dewe, that god wolde pardone me. Wherfore, to
fave them, i wyll be the firft to putte my lyfe in
jeopardy. Whan he had thus fayde, every man
worfhypped hym, and dyvers kneled downe at his
fete, with fore wepyng, and fore fyghes. Than

another honefte burgeffe rofe and fayde, I wyll kepe company with my goffuppe Ewftace: he was called Johan Dayre. Than rofe up Jaques of Wysfant, who was ryche in goodes and herytage; he fayd alfo, that he wolde hold company with his two cofyns in lyke wyfe: fo dyd Peter of Wysfant his brother: and thanne rofe two other; they fayde, they wolde do the fame. Thanne they went and apparelled them as the kyng defyred. Than the captayne went with them to the gate: there was great lamentacyon made, of men, women and chyldren, at their departynge. Than the gate was opyned, and he ysfued out with the vi. burgefses and clofed the gate agayne, fo that they were bytwene the gate and the barryers. Than he fayde to fir Gaultyer of Manny, Sir, i delyver here to you, as captayne of Calys, by the hole confent of all the people of the towne, the fix burgefses; and i fwere to you truely, that they be and were to day mooft honourable, ryche, and mofte notable burgefses of all the towne of Calys. Wherfore, gentyll knyght, i requyre you, pray the kyng to have mercy on theym, that they dye nat. Quod fir Gaultyer, I can nat fay what the kynge wyll do; but i fhall do for them the beft i can. Thanne the barryers were opyned, the fixe burgefses wente towardes the kynge, and the captayne entred agayne into the towne. Whan fir

Gaultier prefented thefe burgefses to the kyng,
they kneled downe, and helde up their handes
and fayde : Gentyll kynge, beholde here, we fixe,
who were burgefses of Calays, and great mar-
chantes, we have brought to you the kayes of the
towne, and of the castell; and we fubmyt oure
felfe clerely into youre wyll and pleafure, to fave
the refydue of the people of Calays, who have
fuffred greate payne. Sir, we befeche youre
grace to have mercy and pytie on us, through
your hygh nobles. Than all the erles and barownes and other that were there wept for pytie.
The kynge loked felly on theym, for greatly he
hated the people of Calys, for the great damages
and displeafures they had done hym on the fee
before. Than he commaunded their heedes to be
ftryken of. Than every man required the kyng
for mercy; but he wolde here no man in that
' behalfe.' Than fir Gaultyer of Manny fayd: A,
noble kynge, for goddes fake refrayne 'your' courage; ye have the name of fouverayne nobles :
therfore nowe do nat a thyng that fhulde blemyffhe
your renome, nor to gyve caufe to fome to fpeke
of you vyllany. Every man woll fay it is a great
cruelty to put to dethe fuche honeft perfons, who
by their owne wylles putte themfelfe into youre
grace to fave their company. Than the kyng
wryed away fro hym, and commaunded to fende

K

for the hangman; and fayde, They of Calys hath caufed many of my men to be flaine, wherfore thefe fhall dye in lyke wyfe. Than the quene, beynge great with chylde, kneled downe, and fore wepynge, fayd : A, gentyll fyr, fith I pafsed the fee in great parell i have defyred nothynge of you; therfore nowe i humbly requyre you, in the honour of the fon of the virgyn Mary, and for the love of me, that ye woll take mercy of thefe fix burgefses. The kynge behelde the quene, and ftode ftyll in a ftudy a fpace, and than fayd : A, dame, i wold ye had ben as nowe in fome other place; ye make fuche requeft to me that i can nat deny you : wherfore i gyve them to you, to do your pleafure with theym. Than the quene caufed them to be brought into her chambre, and made the halters to be taken fro their neckes, and caufed them to be newe clothed, and gave them their dyner at their lefer : and than fhe gave ech of them fixe nobles, and made them to be brought out of thooft in favegarde, and fet at their lyber‑ te. Thus the ftronge towne of Calys was gyven up to kyng Edwarde of Englande the yere of our lorde god m.ccc.xlvi. in the moneth of Auguft." Froisfarts chronicle, vol. i. chap. 133, 144, &c.

To this relation of Froisfart it may not be improper to add the discovery and reflections made, fome years fince, by M. de Brequigny, in confe‑

quence of his refearches in London, relative to
the history of France, as communicated by him
in a memoir to the French academy. (*Mémoires
de litterature de l'académiedes infcriptions,* xxxvii.
528.)

"I fhal not examine the feveral circumftances
of Froisfarts relation, of which he is the only
voucher. Perhaps it may be thought difficult to
reconcile them with certain facts hitherto unknown, but of incontestable authenticity; which
i fhal content myfelf to report.

"The queen, who is fuppofed to have been fo
touched with the mifery of the fix burgefses, whofe
life fhe had faved, did not fail to obtain, a few
days after, the confiscation of the houfes which
John d'Aire, one of them, had posfefsed in Calais.

"The greater part of the other houfes were
given to the Englifh, whom Edward called thither
by his letters of the 12th of Auguft. Calais had
coft him too dear; he felt the importance of fuch
a place too much to neglect anything which might
enfure its prefervation. Even the habitations
which he there granted to his fubjects were not
given without a claufe of felling them to none but
the Englifh.

"It is not, however, necefsary to imagine, as
one commonly believes upon the faith of histo-

rians, that every former posfesfor was driven out, that every Frenchman was excluded; i have feen, on the contrary, a number of French names among thofe of the perfons to whom Edward granted houfes in his new conqueft. But i did not expect to find in the number of thofe who had accepted the favours of the new fovereign, him who appeared the moft likely to disdain them, the famous Euftache de Saint-Pierre.

" By letters, of the 8th of October 1347, two months after the furrender of Calais, Edward gave to Euftache a confiderable penfion, til he fhould provide for him more amply. The mo-tives of this favour are the fervices which he owed to render, either in maintaining good or-der in Calais, or in watching the fafety of that place. Other letters, of the fame date, founded on the fame motives, grant to him and his heirs the greateft part of the houfes and ground which he had posfefsed in that city, and add to them, fur-ther, fome others. That Euftache de Saint-Pierre, the man who is painted to us as immolating him-felf with fo much generofity to the duties of fub-ject and citizen, could confent to acknowlege for fovereign the enemy of his country, to en-gage folemnly to preferve for him that very place which he had fo long defended againft him; in fine, to bind himfelf to him by the ftrongeft tie for a noble mind, the acceptance of a favour, feems to accord little with the high idea hitherto given of his patriotic heroifm.

" His conduct, perhaps, will be attributed to the vexation excited by fome difcontent; and it will be alledged that Froisfart has faid, that Philip did nothing to recompenfe the courage and fidelity of the brave Calefians. But Froisfart was ill-informed. We have many ordinances of Philip, by which he provides for the indemnity of the unfortunate inhabitants of Calais; we have fome which prove that this indemnity took effect; and the kings, his fuccesfors, John II. and Charles V. paid ftill more attention to them.

" It muft therefor be confefsed that the glory of Euftache de Saint-Pierre is fomewhat tarnifhed; and, fince the facts which i expofe appear to impeach it, i fhal make bold to draw from them the conjectures to which they give birth.

" We have feen, by the letters of the Calefians, that their final refolution was to fally out of their walls fword in hand, and to feek, through the Englifh army, death or liberty. It appears evident that Euftache combated this defperate refolution. In the laft council held at Calais, he rofe the firft, and gave his opinion, according to the relation of Froisfart himfelf, to furrender on the conditions which Edward dictated. He faved, by this mean,

the befieged, and fpared the blood of the befieg-
ers; he ferved equally both parties. Edward had
reafon to take this in good part, and was willing to
prove it to him by favours. He had even reafons
to feek to attach to himfelf a man of fo great
weight in the city; and he fucceeded at length
in forcing Euftache to be grateful. This, it appears to me, is what naturally refults from the
combination of the facts which i have ftated."

Page 39.

VIII. Sir David had of his men crete
loss,

With sir Edward at the Nevil-
cross.]

" Whan the kynge of Englande," fays Froisfart,
" had befieged Calays, and lay there, than the
Scottes determyned to make warre into Englande,
and to be revenged of fuch hurtes as they had
taken before; for they fayde than, howe that the
realme of Englande was voyde of men of warre,
for they were, as they fayde, with the kyng of
Englande before Calys, and fome in Bretaygne,
Poyctou, and Gafcoyne. The Frenche kyng dyd
what he coude to ftyre the Scottes to that warre,
to the entent that the kynge of Englande fhulde
breke up his fiege, and retourne to defende his

●wn realme.* The kynge of Scottes made his
ſommons to be at Saynt-Johans-towne, on the ryver of Taye, in Scotlande: thyder came erles,
barownes and prelates of Scotlande; and there

---

* Thus Winton (who has a long chapter,
  " Quhen kyng David paſsyt fra hame
  Till the batell of Durame") :

  " A thowſand and thre hunder yhere
  And ſex and fourty to tha clere,
  The kyng of Frawns ſet hym to raſs
  And ſet a ſege befor Calays,
  And wrate in Scotland till our kyng,
  Specyally be ' tha' praying
  To paſs on were in-till Ingland;
  For he ſayd he ſuld tak on hand
  On other halff thame for to warray,
  Sa upon bathe halfis ſuld thai
  Be ſtraytly ſtad : oure kyng Dawy,
  That wes yhowng, ſtowt, and rycht joly,
  And yharnyd for to ſe fychtyng,
  Grawntyt the kyng off Frawncys yharnyng."

The ſame historian repreſents the allegation of *noue being
at home to let hym the way,* to have occured at a conference
on taking " the pele of Lyddale :"

  " Than confalyd Willame off Dowglas,
  That off weris maſt wyſs than was,
  To turne agayne in thair cuntre;
  He ſayd that with thair honeste

agreed, that, in all hafte posfyble, they fhould entre into Englande. To come in that journey was
defyred Johan of the out iles, who governed the
wylde Scottes; for to hym they obeyed, and to
no many els. He came with a thre thoufande of
the moofte couragyouft people in all that countrey. Whan all the Scottes were asfembled, they
were, of one and other, a fiftye thoufande fyghtynge menne. They coude nat make their asfemble fo fecrete, but that the quene of Englande, who
was as thanne in the marcheffe in the north, about
Yorke, knewe all their dealynge. Than fhe fent
all about for menne, and lay herfelfe at Yorke :
than all men of warre and archers came to Newcastell with the quene. In the meane feafon, the
kyng of Scottes departed fro Saynt-Johannes

> Thai mycht agayne repayr rycht welle
> Syne thai off fors had tane that pelle.
> Bot othir lordis that war by
> Sayd he had fillyd fullyly
> His baggis, and thairis all twme war,
> Thai fai that thai mycht rycht welle fare
> Till Lwndyn, for in Ingland than
> Off gret mycht was lefft na man ;
> For thai fayd all war in Frawns,
> Bot fowteris, fkynneris, or marchawns.
> The Dowglas thare mycht noucht be herd,
> Bot on thaire way all furth thai ferd."

towne, and wente to Donefremelyne the firſte
daye, the nexte daye they paſsed an arme of the
ſee, and ſo came to Eſtermelyne, and than to
Edenbrough. Than they nombred their company, and they were a thre thouſande men of
armes, knyghtes and ſquyers, and a thretie thouſande of other on hackenayes. Than they came
to Rousbourge, the firſt fortreſſe Englyſſh on that
parte; captayne there was ſir Wyllyam Monta-
gue: the Scottes paſsed by, without any asfaut
makynge; and ſo wente forthe brennynge and dis-
troyenge the countrey of Northumberlande; and
their currours ranne 'to Yorke, and brent as
moche as was without the walles, and retourned
agayne to their hooſt, within a dayes journey of
Newcaſtell upon Tyne.

"The quene of Englande, who defyred to defende her contrey, came to Newcaſtell upon Tyne,
and there taryed for her men, who came dayly
fro all partes. Whan the Scottes knewe that the
Englyſſhemen asfembled at Newcaſtell, they drue
thyderwarde, and their currours came rennynge
before the towne; and at their retournynge they
brent certayne ſmall hamelettes thereabout, ſo
that the ſmoke therof came into the towne of
Newcaſtell. Some of the Englyſſhmen wolde a
ysfued out to have fought with them that made
the fyers, but the captayns wolde nat ſuffre theym

to ysfue out. The next day the kynge of Scottes,
with a xl. thoufande men, one and other, came and
lodged within thre lytell Englyffhe myle of Newcastell, in the lande of the lorde Nevyll; and the
kyng fent to them within the towne, that if they
wolde ysfue out into the felde, he wolde fyght
with theym gladly. The lordes and prelates of
Englande fayd, they were content to adventure
their lyves, with the ryght and herytage of the
kynge of Englande their mayster: than they all
ysfued out of the towne, and were in nombre a
twelfe hundred men of armes, thre thoufande
archers, and fevyne thoufande of other with the
Walffhmen. Than the Scottes came and lodged
agaynft theym, nere togyder: than every man
was fette in ordre of batayle. Than the quene
came amonge her men: and there was ordayned
four batayls, one to ayde another. The firfte had
in governaunce the bifhop of Dyrham, and the
lorde Percy: the feconde, the archbysfhoppe of
Yorke, and the lorde Nevyll: the thyrde, the bys-
fhoppe of Lyncolne, and the lorde Mombray: the
fourth, the lorde Edwarde de Bayleule, captayne
of Berwyke, the archbysfhoppe of Canterbury,
and the lorde Rofe: every battayle had lyke nombre after their quantyte. The quene went fro batayle to batayle defyring them to do their devoyre
to defende the honour of her lorde the kyng of

Englande, and in the name of god every man to
be of good hert and courage; promyſyng them
that to her power ſhe wolde remembre them as
well or better as thoughe her lorde the kyng
were there perſonally. Than the quene departed
fro them, recommendyng them to god and to
ſaynt George. Than anone after the bataylles of
the Scottes began to ſet forwarde, and in lyke
manner ſo dyd thenglyſſhmen. Than the archers
began to ſhote on bothe parties; but the ſhot of
the Scottes endured but a ſhort ſpace: but the
archers of Englande ſhot ſo feersly, ſo that whan
the batayls aproched there was a harde batell.
They began at nyne and endured tyll noone. The
Scottes had great axes, ſharpe and harde, and gaue
with them many great ſtrokes, howbeit finally
thenglyſſhmen obtayned the place and vyctorie,
but they loſt many of their men. There were
ſlayne of the Scottes, therle of Sys, therle of Osfre,
the erle of Patnys, therle of Surlant, therle Das-
tredare, therle of Mare, therle Johan Duglas, and
the lorde Alyſaunder Ramſey, who bare the
kynges baner; and dyvers other knightes and
ſquyers. And there the kynge was taken, who
fought valiantly, and was fore hurt: a ſquyer of
Northumberland toke hym, called Johan Coplande; and asſone as he had taken the kynge he
went with hym out of the felde, with viii. of his

fervauntes with hym; and foo rode al that day, tyll
he was a fyftene leages fro the place of the batayle; and at nyght he came to a castell called
Orgulus * . . . The fame day there was alfo taken
in the felde the erle Morette, the erle of Marche,
the lord Wyllyam Duglas, the lorde Robert Ve-
fy, the byſſhoppe of Dadudam, the byſſhoppe of
Saynt ' Andrewes,' and dyvers other knyghtes
and barownes. And there were flayne of one
and other xv. thoufande; and the other faved
themfelfe, as well as they myght. This batell
was befyde Newcaſtell, the yere of our lorde
m.ccc.xlvi. the Saturday next after Saynt My-
chaell.

" Whan the quene of Englande, beynge at
Newcaſtell, underſtode howe the journey was for
her and her men, ſhe than rode to the place
where the batayle had bene ; thanne it was ſhewed her howe the kynge of Scottes was taken by
a fquyer called Johan Coplande, and he hadde
caryed away the kynge no man knewe whyder.
Than the quene wrote to the fquyer, commaund-
yng hym to bring his prifoner . . . and howe he
had nat well done to depart with hym without

* What castle this was does not appear : " *Chaſtell-or-
gueilleux*" is the language of romance. Knyghton fays,
David was led to Bamburgh-castle, then belonging to the
lord Percy.

leave . . . Whan the quenes letter was brought
to Johan Copland, he anſwered and ſayd, that
as for the kyng of Scottes his priſoner, he wolde
nat delyver hym to no man nor woman lyving,
but all onely to the kynge of Englande, his ſove-
rayne lorde: as for the kynge of Scottes, he ſayd,
he ſhuld be ſavely kept, ſo that he wolde gyve
acompte for hym. Thanne the quene ſente letters to the kyng, to Calays, wherby the kyng
was enfourmed of the ſtate of his realme. Than
the kynge ſende incontynent to Johan Coplande,
that he ſhulde come over the ſee to hym, to the
ſiege before Calays. Than the ſame Johan dyd
putte his priſoner in ſave kepynge in a ſtronge
caſtell, and ſo rode through Englande, tyll he
came to Dover; and there toke the ſee, and ar-
ryved before Calays. Whan the kyng of England ſaw the ſquyer, he toke him by the hande
and ſayd, A, welcome, my ſquyer, that by your
valyantneſſe hath taken myne advarſary the kyng
of Scottes. The ſquyer kneled downe and ſayde:
Sir, yf god by his grace hath ſuffred me to take
the king of Scottes by true conqueſt of armes,
ſir, i thynke no man ought to have any envy
thereat; for as wel god maye ſende by his grace
ſuche a fortune to fall to a poore ſquyer, as to a
great lorde: and, ſir, i requyre your grace be
nat myscontent with me, though i dyde nat de-

lyver the kynge of Scottes at the commaunde-
ment of the quene: fir, i holde of you, as myne-
othe is to you, and nat to her, but in all good
maner. The kynge fayd, Johan, the good fer-
vyce that ye have done, and your valyantneſſe is
ſo moche worthe, that hit muſt countervayle your
trespaſſe, and be taken for your excuſe; and
ſhame have they that bere you any yvell wyll
therfore. Ye ſhall retourne agayne home to your
houſe; and thanne my pleaſure is that ye delyver
your priſoner to the quene my wyfe: and in a re-
warde i asſygne you, nere to your houſe, where as
ye thynke beſt yourſelfe, fyve hundred pounde
ſterlyng of yerely rent, to you and your heyres for
ever: and here i make you ſquyer for my body.*
Thanne, the thyrde day, he departed, and retourned agayne into Englande; and whan he
came home to his owne houſe, he asſembled toguyder his frendes and kynne, and ſo they toke
the kynge of Scottes, and rode with hym to the
cytie of Yorke, and there, fro the kyng his lorde,
he preſented the kynge of Scottes to the quene,
and excuſed hym ſo largely, that the quene and
her counſell were content. Than the quene . . .

* The king made him a banneret. The £500 a year was
to be paid out of the customs of London and Berwick till the
land could be provided. See Stows *Annales*, 1592, p. 375.
Fœdera, v. 5.

departed fro Yorke towardes London. Than she
fette the kynge of Scottes in the ftronge towre
of London, and therle Morette, and all other
prifoners; and fette good kepyng over them."
(Vol. i. cc. 137, &c.)

Froisfart, in this narrative, has embraced for
truth fome confiderable errors. In the firft place,
that the queen was not in the north at this period,
nor had any concern whatever in the command
or direction of the army, is clear from the filence
of our own contemporary or moft ancient historians: neither was fhe vice gerent or warden of the
kingdom, as he feems to fuppofe. Secondly, the
battle was not "befyde Newcastell," but between
Durham and a village called Kirk-Merrington,
near twenty miles off. It is called *the battle of Nevils-crofs*, from an ancient ftone-crofs erected by
one of that family, about a mile from Durham,
and demolifhed, by fome puritanical enthufiafts, in
1569, near which was probably the heat or conclufion of the fight.* The purfuit, according to
Stow, continued as far as Prudhow and Cor-
bridge, on the north fide of the Tyne.

John Copland, in taking king David prifoner,

---

* Modern writers fuppofe this crofs to have been erected
in confequence of the battle; whereas it was clearly a well-
known ftation at the time.

(according to Wynton) had two of his teeth
knocked out by that monarch :

> " Jhon off Cowpland thare tuk the kyng,
> Off forfs noucht yholdyne in that takyng;
> The kyng twa teth owt off his hevyd
> With a dynt off a knyff hym revyd."

" This battell," fays Stow, " was fought on the
feventeenth of October [1346]. The prifoners
were conveyed to London about Chriftmaffe, David le Brufe except, which might not travell by
reafon of two deadly woundes in his head with ar-
rowes; but the fecond of Jannuary he was brought
up, and conveyed from Weftminfter to the tower .
of London, in fight of all the people, and there
lodged in the blacke nooke of the fayde tower,
neere to the conftables guard, there to be kept."*
(*Annales*, 1592, p. 374.) That Edward Baliol

* David was actually delivered, at York, by *Ralph de
Nevill* to Thomas de Rokeby, fherif of Yorkfhire, and by
him, on the 2d of January, 1346-7, delivered into the
custody of John Darcy, conftable of the tower of London.
(*Fœdera*, v. 539.) That he was taken by Copland is certain ; but the conteft or transaction between this gentleman
and the queen, though adopted by Carte, Hume, and other
modern historians, feems nothing more than an ill-founded
report, not to believe it the invention of Froisfart, to do honour to his country-woman.

had fome command in the Englifh army at the battle of Durham is highly probable, but it cannot be accurately afcretained. See lord Haileses *Annals of Scotland*, ii. 213. Hutchinfons *History of Durham*, ii. 337.

" Cuthbert of Dorem" (p. 44) is faint Cuthbert, concerning whom fee the laft-mentioned work (i. 20).

Page 45.

IX. How king Edwarde with his menze Met with the Spaniardes in the see.]

"In the fommer ' 1350,' variance rifing betweene the fleets of England and Spaine, the Spaniards befet the Brytaine fea, with 44 great fhippes of warre, with the which they funke ten Englifh fhips comming from Gascoigne towardes Englande, after they had taken and fpoyled them, and thus their former injuries being revenged, they entred into Sluce in Flanders.

" King Edwarde underftanding heereof, furnifhed his navie of fiftie fhippes and pinaces, forecafting to meete with the Spaniards in their returne, having in his company the prince of Wales, the earles of Lancaster, North-hampton, Warwicke, Salisburie, Arundale, Huntington, Glocester, and other barons and knightes with their fervants and archers, and upon the feaft of the decolation of S.

L

John, about evenſong time, the navies mette at
Winchelſea, where the great Spaniſh vesſels ſur-
mounting our ſhips and ſoyſtes, like as castles to
cotages, ſharply asſailed our men ; the ſtones and
quarels flying from the tops, ſore and cruelly
wounded our men, who no leſſe buſie to fight
aloofe with launce and ſword, and with the fore-
ward manfully defend themſelves ; at length our
archers pearced their arbalisters with a further
retch then they could ſtrike againe, and thereby
compelled them to forſake their place, and cauſed
other fighting from the hatches to ſhade themſelves with tables of the ſhips, and compelled them
that threw ſtones from the toppes, ſo to hide them,
that they durſt not ſhew their heades, but tumble
downe: then our men entring the Spaniſh vesſels
with ſwords and halberds, kill thoſe they meete,
within a while make voyde the vesſels, and fur-
niſh them with Engliſh-men, until they, beeing
beſette with darkeneſſe of the night, could not
discerne the 27 yet remaining untaken: our men
caſt anker, ſtudying of the hoped battell, ſuppo-
ſing nothing finiſhed whileſt any thing remained
undone, dreſsing the wounded, throwing the mi-
ſerable Spaniards into the ſea, refreſhing themſelves with victuals and ſleepe, yet committing
the vigilant watche to the armed bande. The
night overpaſsed, the Engliſh-men prepared (but

in vain) to a new battel; but when the funne began to appeare, they viewing the feas, coulde per-
ceive no figne of refistance; for 27 fhips flying
away by night, left 17 fpoiled in the evening to
the kings pleafure, but againft their will.

" The king returned into England with victorie and triumph; the king preferred there 80
noble ympes to the order of knighthood, greatly
bewayling the loffe of one, to wit, fyr Richard
Goldesborough, knight." Stows *Annales*, 1592,
p. 385.

Page 48.

X. How GENTILL SIR EDWARD, WITH HIS
    GRETE ENGINES,
    WAN WITH HIS WIGHT MEN THE CAS-
    TELL OF GYNES.]

The beft hiftorical account of this capture feems
to be that given by Stow; Froisfart and Fabian
but flightly mentioning it.

" About the beginning of Januarie [1352],
the Frenchmen being occupied about the repayring of the walles of Guifnes towne, being afore
that time deftroyed by the Englifhmen, fome men
of armes of Caleis, underftanding their doings,
devifed how they might overthrow the worke, in
this fort. There was an archer named John
Dancafter, in prifon in the caftell of Guifnes,

before that time taken, who not having wherewith to pay his raunfome, was let lofe, with condition that hee fhould worke there among the
Frenchmen. This fellow chanced to lye with a
laundres, a ftrumpet, & learned of her where
beyond the principall ditch, from the bottome of
the ditch, there was a wall made of two foote
broade, ftretching from the rampiers to the
brimme of the ditch within forth, fo that being
covered with water it could not be feene, but not
fo drowned, but that'a man going aloft thereon,
fhould not bee wette paft the knees, it being
made for the ufe of fifhers ; and therefore in the
middeft it was discontinued for the fpace of two
foote: and fo the archer (his harlot fhewing it to
him) meafured the heyght of the wall with a
threede. Thefe thinges thus knowen, one day
flipping downe from the wall, he pafsed the ditch
by that hidden wal, and, lying hidde in the marfh
til evening, came in the night neare unto Caleis,
where tarying for the cleare day, hee then went
into the towne (for elfe he might not) ; here he
inftructed them that were greedie of pray to ' fcale
the castell, and' howe they might enter the fame :
they caufed ladders to be made to the length by
the archer appointed. Thirtie men confpired to-
gither, clothing themfelves in blacke armour
without any brightneffe, went to the castel, by

the guiding of the faid John de Dancaster, and
climing the wall with their ladders, they flewe the
watchmen, and threwe them downe headlong befide the wall: after this, in the hall they flew
many, whome they found unarmed, playing at the
cheffe and hazard. Then they brake into the
chambers and turrets, upon the ladies and knights
that lay there afleepe, and fo were masters of all
that was within: and fhutting all their prifoners
into a ftrong chamber, being bereft of all their
armour, they tooke oute the Englifhmen that had
bene taken the yeere before, and there kept in
prifon; and after they had relieved them well
with meate and drinke, they made them guardens
over them that had them in custodie: and fo they
wanne all the fortreffes of the castell, unknowen
to them that were in the towne (appointed to
overfee the repayring of the broken walles) what
had happened to them within the castell. In the
morning they commaunded the workemen in the
towne to ceafe from their workes, who thereupon,
perceiving that the castell was wonne, ftreight-
wayes fledde; and the newe *Castilians* fuffered the
ladies to depart on horfebacke, with their apparell,
writings and muniments, where[by] they ought
to hold their fees: and the fame day there came
from Caleis to their ayde fuch perfons as they fent
for, by whofe ayde they kept the castell: and
about three of the clocke there came two knights,

fent from the earle of Guifnes, who, demanding a
truce, willed to know of them that were thus
entred the castell, who they were, to whom they
belonged, and by whofe authority they kept the
castell, fo taken in the time of truce; whereunto
they anfwered, that being intruded, they woulde
not declare to any man their purpofe, till they
had tryed a longer posfesfion: and therefore, on
faint Mawrice day the abbot, (the king being
bufie in parliament) 'fome' Frenchmen, being fent
from the fayde earle of Guifnes, declared, how in
prejudice of the truce the fayd castell was taken,
and therefore by right of mutuall faith it ought
to be reftored unto them. The king anfwered,
that without his knowledge that enterprife was
made, and therefore he gave commandement to
his fubjectes that none of them fhould deteyne
the castell of 'Guifnes,' but deliver it unto the
lawfull lordes thereof. The mesfengers being returned home, and reporting what they had done,
the earle of Guifnes commeth to the castell, demanding of them within, as at other times, in
whofe names they kept it; who conftantly af-
firming that they kept it in the name of John
Dancaster, hee required to knowe if the fame John
were the king of Englands liegeman, or would
obey him; who anfwering that hee knewe not
what mesfengers had beene in England, the earle
offered for the castell, befides all the treafure

found in it, many thoufands of crownes or posfesfions for exchange, and a perpetuall peace with
the king of Fraunce. To this they anfwered, that
before the taking of that castell they were Eng-
liſhmen by nation, but by their demerites ban-
niſhed for the peace of the king of England,
wherefore the place which they thus helde they
would willingly fell or exchange, but to none
fooner then to their naturall king of England, to
whom, they faid, they would fell their castell to
obtaine their peace: but if he would not buy it,
then they would fell it to the king of France, or
to whomfoever would give the moft for it.

"The earle being thus ſhifted of from them,
the king of England bought it in deede, and fo had
that place which hee greatly defired." *Annales,*
1592, p. 388.

L. 5. *Both the lely and the lipard.*] The author
alludes to the armorial enfigns of the two kingdoms. That the LIONS in the Engliſh ſhield were
originally LEOPARDS is a faȼt not to be disputed.
Thus Langtoft, as rendered by his ingenious translator, Robert of Brunne, ſpeaking of the battle of
Falkirk:

"Thei fauh kynges banere, raumpand thre
LEBARDES."

See alfo Draytons *Poly-Olbion,* fong the eleventh,
and the learned Seldens illustrations.

GLOSSARY.

Ailed. *p.* 41.

Aire. *p.* 14. *heir.*

Albidene. *p.* 34. *from time to time, one after another? The word* bidene *is generally ufed for* prefently, in a fhort time, by and by, *none of which fenfes feem to fuit the prefent text: and the meaning is as doubtful in other places. Thus, in the ancient metrical romance of* Ywaine and Gawin, *MS.*

> " *His hert he has fet* albydene,
> *Whar himfelf dar noght be fene.*"

Again:

> " *The king himfelf & als the quene,
> & other knightes* albidene.*"

Again:

> " *Now fal you have noght bot their awin,
> That is the half of* al bydene.*"

See Bidene. Bydene.

Alblaft. *p.* 16. (*more properly* Arblaft; arcbalefte, *F.* Arcu-balifta, *L.*) *a crofs-bow; put in the text for the* arbalifter *or crofs-bow-man. Fabian ufes* Arblasters *for crofs-bows (fee before,* p. 73*); as Stow does* Arbalisters, *in* p. 140, *for crofs-bow-men. Thus alfo Robert of Brunne:*

> " *That fauh an* alblastere, *a quarelle lete he flie.*"

Ald. *p.* 8. *old.*

Allane. *p.* 44. *alone.*

Alls. *p.* 4. *alſo.*   Als. *p.* 3. *l.* 4. *as.—l.* 19. *alſo.*

Alweldand. *p.* 28. *all-wielding, all-governing.*

Are. *p.* 31. *ere, before.*

Aſcry. herd aſcry. *p.* 14. *heard it ſpoken, cryed, reported, or proclaimed.*

Asſoyl. *p.* 12. *abſolve.*

At. *p.* 2. *to.*

Avance. *p.* 39. Avaunce. *p.* 4. *advance.*

Bade. *p.* 20. *abode.*

Balde. *p.* 49. *bold.*

Baldely. *p.* 20. Baldly. *p.* 11. *boldly.*

Bale. *p.* 1. *evil, miſery, ſorrow.*

Ban. *p.* 38. *curſe.*

Bare. *p.* 26. *boar.* See the note.

Bavere. *p.* 8. *Bavaria.*

Bede. *pp.* 6, 19. *offer.*

Beld. *p.* 27. *refuge, help, protection.*

Beme. *p.* 16. *Bohemia.*

Bere. *p.* 24. *bier.* broght on bere. *dead.*

Bere-bag. *pp.* 7, 41. *bag-bearer, carry-ſack, wallet-man. Froiſſart, deſcribing the manners of the Scots during their military expeditions, ſays:* " *They cary with them none other purveyance, but on their horſe bitwene the ſaddyll and the pannell they truſſe a brode plate of metall, and behynde the ſaddyl they wyll have* a lytel ſacke, *full of ootemele, to the entent, that whan they have eaten of the ſodden fleſſhe, than they ley this plate on the fyre, and tempre a lytel of the otemele, & whan the plate is hote they caſt of the thyn paſte theron, and ſo make a lytle cake in maner of a crakenell or byſket, and that they eate to comforte withall theyr ſtomaks.*

Wherfore it is no great merveile though they make greatter journeys than other people do." (*Vol. i. chap. 17.*)

John of Hexham observes that the field where the battle of the standard was fought, in 1138, *obtained the name of* Baggamor, *from the facks or wallets left thereon by the enemy.* (X fcrip. *p.* 262.)

Befy. *p.* 2. *bufy, active, officious.*

Betes. *p.* 7. *l.* 9. *beats, walks up and down: fee* batre les rues, batre le pavé, *in Cotgraves dictionary.*

Betes. *p.* 7. *l.* 12. *amends, heals, cures.*

Bid. *p.* 1. *offer, prefer, put up.*

Bidene (*or* All bidene). *p.* 11. *prefently, immediately.—p.* 37. *in procefs of time, or, perhaps, one after another ?* See Al-bidene. Bydene.

Biforn. *p.* 12. *before.*

Big. *p.* 29.

Big. *p.* 35. *build, erect.* Bigged him. *p.* 33. *lodged him, pofted himfelf, made his dwelling or habitation, taken up his refidence.*

Biging. *p.* 7. *dwelling, habitation.*

Biker. *p.* 20. *bicker, fkirmifh.—p.* 51. *asfail, attack.*

Bilevid. *p.* 10. *was left, remained.—p.* 30. *are left, are remaining.*

Blin. *p.* 21. *ceafe.* Blinned. *p.* 21. *ceafed.*

Bone. *pp.* 1, 15. *prayer, requeft.*

Bot. *p.* 6. *both;* as we fhould probably read.

Bot. *p.* 13. *but.*

Bote. *p.* 15. *boot, amends, remedy, help.*

Boun, *p.* 51. Boune. *p.* 24. *ready prepared.*

Boure. *p.* 35. *habitation.*

Brade. *p.* 20. *broad.*

Brak. *p.* 29. *broke.*

Brandes, *p.* 29. *fire brands, things on fire.*

Brems, *p.* 22. *perhaps* Brenis, *corslets; as in the ancient Scot-ish metrical romance of the* Aunter of fir Gawane *(a MS. in the editors posfesfion, furreptitiously printed, in* 1792, *by* John Pinkerton) :

> " *Shene fheldes were fhred,*
> *Bright* brenes *by bled.*"

See, alfo, the glosfary to Bp. Douglases Virgil, *in the word* Byrnie.

Brend. *p.* 10. *burned.*

Brene, *p.* 23. *burn.*

Brid. *p.* 4. *bird.*

Brig. *p.* 7. *bridge.*

Brin. *p.* 10. *burn.*

Bud. *p.* 10. *behoved, muft.*

Burgafe. *p.* 37. *burgefses.*

Burghes. *p.* 7. *boroughs.*

Burjafe. *p.* 18. *burgefses.*

Bufk, *p.* 7. *hye.*

Bute. *p.* 1. *See* Bote.

Bydene. *p.* 15. *after or beyond them ? The word occurs, with an apparently fimilar fenfe, in the* Aunter of fir Gawane :

> " *Bothe the kyng and the quene,*
> *And al the* doughti bydene."

Again :

> " *They fhullen dye on a day, the* doughty bydene."

Its etymology is uncertain ; the one, at leaft, conjectured by fome (i. e. by the even, *as* belive, *a term of fimilar fignifi-*

cation, they think, comes from by le eve,) *is altogether unsa-tisfactory. See* Albidene. Bidene.

Caitefes. *p.* 4. *caitifs, wretches.*

Cant. *p.* 30. *brisk, in high spirits: the word* canty *is still used in Scotland with this sense.*

Cantly. *p.* 20. *briskly.*

Clerkes. *p.* 40. *learned men.*

Clip. *p.* 23. *embrace.*

Come. *p.* 9. *came.*

Confort. *p.* 13. *comfort.*

Conig. *p.* 37. *coney, rabbit.*

Covaitife. *p.* 4. *covetousness.*

Cumand. *p.* 10. *commanded.*

Cumen. *p.* 18. *come.*

Dale. *pp.* 1, 2. *valley, used metonymically for the world or earth, which is still frequently termed* a vale of misery.

Dare. *p.* 2. *stare, as one terrifyed or amazed?* Dareand. *p.* 3. *stareing,* &c.

Ded. *p.* 34. *deed.*

Dele. *p.* 9. *quantity.*

Dene. *p.* 23. *den, habitation ?*

Dere. *p.* 2. *hurt, harm, injury, trouble, vexation.*

Dere. *p.* 3. *hurt, harm, vex,* &c.

Dern. *p.* 2. *cruel, severe.*

Did. *p.* 20. *caused, made.*

Dight. *p.* 4. *dressed.—pp.* 19, 22, 50. *dressed, addressed, prepared, made ready.* Dightes. *p.* 27. *addresses, prepares. So, in the old romance of* Syr Degore :
　　" *All thyng redy to souper he* dyghte."

Dint. *p.* 2. *stroke.* Dintes. *p.* 23. *strokes.*

Do. *p.* 47. *caufe, make.*

Dole. *p.* 4. *forrow, grief.*—*p.* 31. *fhare, portion.*

Domp. *p.* 47. *plunge, plump, fall, or be thrown.*

Dongen. *p.* 29. *dung, thrown.*

Done. *p.* 2. *do, caufe.*—*p.* 39. *caufed, made.*

Dowt. *p.* 23. *doubt, be doubtful or fufpicious.*

Dray. *p.* 35. *noife, riotous mirth;* desroy, *F. So, in a cele-*
brated Scotifh poem:

"*Was never in Scotland hard nor fene*
Sic danfing and deray."

Drefce. *p.* 1. *drefs, addrefs, direct.*

Drewris. *p.* 31. *jewels, ornaments of drefs, things rich and va-*
luable. Thus, in the ancient metrical romance of Ywaine
and Gawin :

"*The lady made ful meri chere*
Sho was al dight with drewris der."

Eghen. *p.* 29. *eyes.*

Er. *p.* 4. *are.*

Ertou. *p.* 31. *art thou.*

Es. *p.* 2. *is.*

Eth. *p.* 20. *eafy.*

Everilka. *p.* 51. *every.*

Faine. *p.* 50. *eager.*

Faire, *pp.* 16, 29. *fairly.*

Famen. *p.* 25. *foemen, enemies.*

Fand. *p.* 10. *found.*

Fare. *p.* 2. *l.* 5. *go, fpeed.*

Fare. *p.* 5. *l.* 16.

Felde. *p.* 16. *field.*

Fele. *p.* 8. *many, feveral.*

Fell. *p.* 19. *fierce, cruel, wicked, malicious.*

Felony. *p.* 27. *villainy, wickedneſs, malice, treaſon, treachery, mischief.*

Fer. *p.* 20. *far.*

Ferd. *pp.* 13, 18. *fared, went.*

Ferd. *pp.* 15, 16. (*l.* 2.) *feared, afraid.*

Ferd. *p.* 14. *l.* 24. Ferde. *p.* 14. *fear.*

Fere. *p.* 24. *companion.*

Ferr. *p.* 46. *farer, further. The line, however, ſhould, pro-bably, be read:*

  "Flit *might thai no ferr.*"

Ferrum. o ferrum. *p.* 29. *afar off.*

File. *pp.* 31, 36. *a coward, perhaps, or worthleſs perſon. The word is alſo uſed by Robert Brunne:*

  "*David at that while was with Edward the kyng,*
  Zit avanced he that file *untille a faire thing.*"

Hearne, at random, explains it by "fool, thread, tri-fle."

Fine. *p.* 46. *end.*

Fleand. *p.* 29. *fleeing, flying.*

Flemid. *p.* 3. *baniſhed.*

Flit. *p.* 46. *remove.*

Fode. freely fode. *p.* 25. *freely-fed, gently-nurtured, well-bred (ſub. youth, or young perſon); from the Saxon Foe-dan, to feed; a frequent expresſion in old metrical romances. Thus, in that of* Tristrem:

  "*Her forwen and her care*
  Thai with that frely fode.*"

Again, in Ywayne *and* Gawin:

  "*My daughter, fayreſt* fode olyve.*"

It is likewife ufed by Winton:
  " Syne Saxon and the Scottis blude
  Togyddyr is in yhon frely fwde."

Fold. *p.* 35.

Fonde. *p.* 39. *attempt, endeavour, ftrive.*

Fone. *p.* 7. *few.*

Forthi. *p.* 29. *therefor, for that reafon.*

Forward. *p.* 43. *promife, covenant.*

Founded. *p.* 2. *went, iffued.*

Fra. *p.* 3. *from.*

Franceis. *p.* 31. *Frenchman.*

Frankis. *p.* 22. *franks,* " *a denomination of French money,*
  anfwering at prefent to the livre Tournois."

Frek. *pp.* 2, 15. *perhaps, ready, eager. The word* frakly
  (nimbly, fwiftly, haftyly) is ufed by bifhop Douglas.

Frely. *p.* 25. *freely. See* Fode.

Frith. *p.* 9. *wood.*

Fro. *p.* 28. *from, from the time that.*

Fun. *p.* 38. *found.*

Funden. *p.* 36. *found.*

Fune. *p.* 7. *few.*

Fyne. *p.* 50.

Gaf. *p.* 16. *gave.*

Gafe. *p.* 7. *goes.*

Gafte. haly gafte. *p.* 13. *holy ghoft.*

Gate. *p.* 28. *way.*

Gaudes. *p.* 5. *tricks. So Winton:*
  " But this kyng Edward all wyth gawdys
  Knakkyd Robert the Brws wyth frawdis."

Geneuayfe. *p.* 32. *Genoefe.*

Geder. *p.* 48. *gather, meet.*

Ger. *p.* 27. *caufe.* Gert. *p.* 9. *caufed.*

Geftes. *p.* 50. *guefts.*

Get. *p.* 7. *an interjection of contempt.*

Giff. *p.* 16. *give.*

Gile. *p.* 5. *guile, deceit, treachery.*

Gle. *p.* 10. *mirth.*

Gode. *p.* 11. *goods, property.*

Grame. *p.* 18. *harm, mischief.*

Graytheft. *p.* 28. *readyeft, neareft, beft.*

Gude. *p.* 6. *good.*

Gude. *p.* 12. *goods.*

Hald. *p.* 9. *hold.*

Halely. *p.* 16. *wholely.*

Haly. *p.* 13. *See* Gaft.

Hat. *p.* 16. *was called.*

Haved. Haves. *p.* 42. *had, has.*

Hele. *p.* 49. *health.*

Hele. *p.* 22. *hide, conceal.* Helis. *p.* 22. *hide, conceal.*

Hend. *p.* 9. *hand.*

Hende. *p.* 22. *kind, gentle.*

Hent. *p.* 22. *caught.*

Here. *p.* 46. *hair.*

Heres. *p.* 33. *hear.*

Heried. *p.* 27. *harryed, fpoiled, ravaged, plundered. Jefus Chrift, after his refurrection, made a hoftile defcent or irrup-tion into hell, and, armed with his crofs, (the devils, terri-fyed perhaps by fo unufual a weapon, not daring to oppofe him,) carryed off a number of damned fouls. See a curious*

M

representation of this transaction in Hearnes edition of J. de Fordun Scotichronicon, *p.* 1403.

Hernes. *p.* 10. *brains.*

Hetes. *p.* 7. *threatens.—p.* 24. *promises.*

Heviddes. *p.* 16. *heads.*

Hevidles. *p.* 12. *headless.*

Hevyd. *p.* 10. *head.*

Hight. *p.* 26. *was called.*

Hinde. *p.* 42. *gentle, courteous.*

Hire. *p.* 12.

Hoved. *p.* 11. *hovered, remained.*

Hurdis. *p.* 46. *ropes?*

Ilk. *p.* 11. Ilka. *p.* 2. *each, every.* Ilk one. *p.* 37. *every one.*

Ine. *p.* 29. *eyes.*

Ines *p.* 13. *inn, lodging, residence.*

Inogh. *p.* 18. *enough.*

Japes. *p.* 13. *tricks, jeers, mocks.*

Jornay. *p.* 9. *journey, expedition:* journée, F.

Kaitefs. *p.* 20. *caitifs, knaves.*

Kayes. *p.* 7. *keys.*

Kayfer. *p.* 8. *emperor.*

Ken. *p.* 21. *know.—p.* 23. *teach.* Kend. *p.* 42. *taught.*

Kene. *p.* 6. *keen, sharp, fierce, cruel.* pp. 19, 20. *bold.*

Kid. *p.* 4. *known.*

Kirk. *p.* 4. *church.*

Kirtell. *p.* 36. *tunic or waistcoat.*

Kith. *p.* 20. *shew.*

Kouth. *p.* 20. *could, knew, was master of.*

Kumly. *p.* 30. *comely.*

Kun. *p.* 38. *can, knows how.*

Lare. *p.* 18. *doctrine.*

Lat. *p.* 30. *let.*

Law. *p.* 30. *low.*

Laykes. *p.* 10. *plays, sports, pastimes.*

Ledeing. *p.* 36. *leading, management.*

Lele. *p.* 9. *true.* Lely. *p.* 28, *truely.*

Lely. *p.* 47. Lely-flowre. *p.* 16. *the lilly or flower-de-luce:* (*"floure de lice"*, *p.* 14. fleur de lis, *F.*) *the national or royal shield of France being a blue field, powdered with those flowers, since reduced to three. See p.* 151.

Len. *p.* 51. *lend;* i. e. *lend him grace.*

Lend. *p.* 9. *stayed, remained. So in* Ywaine and Gawin :
> " *Sir* Ywaine *wald no lenger* lend,
> *But redies him fast for to wend.*"

Lended. *p.* 36.

Lere. *pp.* 20, 23. *learn, teach.* At lere them. *to learn or teach themselves.*—*p.* 36. *learn.* Lesed. *p.* 18. *taught.*

Let. *p.* 40. *hinder.* Letes. *p.* 40. *stops, hinders.* Lett. *p.* 10. *hindered, put a stop to.*

Leve. *p.* 18. *believe.* Leves. *p.* 12. *believe.*

Leved. *p.* 44.

Levid. *p.* 3. *left.*

Lif *p.* 14. *live.* Lifes. *p.* 12. *lives.*

Lig. *p.* 29. *lye.* Ligand. *p.* 37. *lying.* Ligges. *p.* 12. *lye.*

Lift. *p.* 23.

Lithes. *p.* 1. *listen, attend, hear, hearken.*

Live. *p.* 5. *life.*

Lout. *p.* 23. *honour; properly to bow.*—*pp.* 30, 44. *bow down, stoop.*

Lystens. *p.* 36. *listen.*

Ma. *p.* 3. *more.*

Main. *p.* 25. Mainc. *p.* 5. *corporal strength, force.* main and mode. *p.* 25. *body and mind.*

Maistri. *p.* 12. *force, power.*

Maked. *p.* 3. Makked. *p.* 27. *made.*

Mane. *p.* 12. *moan.*

Mafe. *p.* 35. *make.*

Mafte. *p.* 13. *moft.*

Mawgre. *p.* 3. *defpite.*

Mede. *p.* 3, 24, 51. *reward.*

Mekil. *p.* 20. Mekill. *p.* 5. *much, great.*

Menid. *p.* 18. *meant, intended.*

Menzè. *pp.* 5, 13. *followers, retinue:* mesnie, *F.*

Middelerd. *p.* 1. *the earth.*

Misliked. *p.* 28. *disliked.*

Misliking. *p.* 28. *dislike, displeafure.*

Mo. *p.* 8. *more.*

Mode. *p.* 25. *mind, fpirit. See* Main.

Mody. *p.* 19. *brave, fpirited.*

Mold. *p.* 34. *earth.*

Mone. *p.* 1. *moon.*

Moné. *p. money.*

Mot. *p.* 3. *may.*

Mote. *p.* 23. *meet.*

Mun. *p.* 3. *muft.*

Nakers. *p.* 16. *tymbals; a fpecies of martial mufic adopted from the Saracens.*

Nane. *p.* 12. *none.*

Naverne. *p.* 16. *Navarre.*

Ne. *p.* 6. *nor.*

Neghed. *p.* 45. *nighed, approached, drew near to.*

Nerr. *p.* 46. *near.*

Noght. *p.* 2. *l.* 8. *not.*—*p.* 10. *nothing.*—es noght at hide.
p. 2. *l.* 12. *it fignifies nothing to conceal it.*

Nokes. *p.* 26. *nooks, corners.*

Nomen. *p.* 43. *took.*

Nowther. *p.* 30. *neither.*

Ogaines, *p.* 2. Ogains. *p.* 14. *againft.*

Ogayn. *p.* 2. *again.*

Olive. *p.* 19. *alive.*

Omang. *p.* 30. *among.*

Or. *p.* 10. *before.*

Oway. *p.* 19. *away.*

Palet. *p.* 31. *head, fcul, crown, pate. Pinkerton, in one of
the miferable pieces of guefs-work, he is pleafed to call a*
gloffary, *interprets* " BREAK your PALLAT,"—" CUT
your THROAT."

Pall. *p.* 30. *fine cloth, ufed for the robes of kings and princes.*
   " *Sometime let gorgeous Tragedy,*
   In fceptred pall *come fweeping by.*"
*The word, at laft, became fignificant rather of the fhape than
of the quality of the garment, as we fometimes read of " a
pall of white filk."* (*See Langhams letter from Killing-
worth,* 1575.) *It is now confined to the ornamental cover-
ing of black velvet ufed in funeral-proceffions.*

Pay. *p.* 8. *content, fatisfaction.*

Pelers. *p.* 6. *pillars.*

Pencell. *p.* 28. *a fmall ftreamer.*

Pere. *p.* 8. *peer, equal.*

Pine. *pp.* 29, 50. *pain.*

Pitaile. *p.* 28. *foot-foldiers:* pitaille, *F.*

Plate. *p.* 28. *maii, armour, as breaſt-plate, back-plate. Thus*
Spenſer (Faerie queene, V. viii. 29):
     " *So, forth he came all in a coat of* plate."

Pleyn tham. *p.* 29. *complain.*

Polled. *p.* 31. *ſhaven.*

Povre. *p.* 12. *poor :* pauvre, *F.*

Preſe. *p.* 5. *preſs, croud.*

Preſt. *p.* 20. *ready.*

Priked. *p.* 6. *riden.*

Priſe. *p.* 2. *price, value.—p.* 14. *prize, praiſe, eſteem.*

Proved. *p.* 27. *ſtrove, tryed.*

Purvay. *p.* 14. *provide, prepare.*

Quell. *p.* 4. *kill.*

Quite. *p.* 31. *quit.*

Railed. *p.* 16. *ſet, placed.*

Rapely. *p.* 24. *briſkly, haſtyly, ſoon, quickly.*

Rapes. *p.* 37. *ropes.*

Rathly. *p.* 29. *ſoon, quickly.—p.* 24. *eagerly, readyly.*

Raw. *p.* 16. *row.*

Rede. *p.* 9. *advice, counſel.*

Rede. *p.* 46. *adviſe, counſel.*

Redles. *p.* 22.

Ren. *p.* 34. *run.*

Reſe. *p.* 28.

Reved. *p.* 12. *robbed, taken away.*

Rig. *p.* 29. *back.*

Rightwis. *p.* 30. *righteous, juſt.*

Riveling. *p.* 7. *This word is uſed, as an adjective, by Chaucer,*
     in his Romant of the roſe, *with the ſignification of wrinkled:*
         " *Or botis* riveling *as a gipe ;*"
     whence it may be ſuppoſed to mean, in the text, a man ſhri-

*eled or wrinkled with hunger. It is, however, found to
occur, as a substantive, in Robert Mannyngs translation of
Peter Langtofts chronicle:*
"*Thou scabbed Scotte, thi nek thi hotte, the develle it breke,*
It salle be hard to here Edward ageyn the speke.
He salle the ken, our lond to bren, & werre biginne,
Thou getes no thing, bot thi rivelyng, *to hang ther inne.*"
*Its meaning, at the same time, is still uncertain; but unless
it exist, in other passages, as an adjective, it is most absurdly,
and, at any rate, imperfectly, interpreted by Hearne, "turn-
ing in and out, wriggling." See* Rugh-fute, *below.*

Rode. *p.* 25. *rood, crofs.*

Romance. *pp.* 26, 33. *story; any historical relation in vulgar
poetry. The word is frequently used by Robert of Brunne
in the sense of a common history, as well as for his French
original.*

Rugh fute. *p.* 7. *rough-foot, rough-footed. Our author, pro-
bably, alludes to a sort of shoes, called* rullions, *made by the
Scots from the raw hide with the hair on. They are mentioned
by bishop Douglas, in his "sevynth booke of Eneados:"*
"*There left fute and al thare leg was bare,*
Ane rouch rilling *of* raw hyde and of hare
The tothir fute coverit wele and knyt."
Blind Harry (about 1460) *makes young Selby taunt his hero,
Wallace, in the following terms:*
"*He callyt on hym, and said, Thou Scot, abyde!*
Quha dewill the grathis in so gay a wyde?
Ane Ersche mantill it was thi kynd to wer,
A Scotts thewittil undyr thi belt to ber,
Rouch rowlyngs *apon thi harlot fete,*
Giff me thi knyff, quhat dois thi ger sa mete?"

The word Rewelyngs, *in the sense of rullions or brogues, is repeatedly used by Andrew of Wyntown.*

Sad. *p.* 18. *serious, grave, solemn.*

Saine. *p.* 5. *say.*

Sakles. *p.* 6. *guiltless, blameless, innocent.*

Sal. *p.* 18. *shall.*

Saltou. *p.* 46. *shalt thou.*

Salve. *p.* 18.

Sare. *p.* 2. *sore.*

Sari. *p.* 29. Sary. *p.* 4. *sorry.*

Saul. *p.* 8. *soul.*

Sawes. *p.* 18. *sayings, discourses.*

Sawls. *p.* 21. *souls.*

Schac. *p.* 14. *shake.*

Schawes. *p.* 48. *woods.*

Scheltron. *p.* 20. *a body of foot, in a compact circle ; so called, it would seem, from the appearance of their* shields; *which, together with that of their spear-points, might also give occasion to the epithet* shene *or* shining. *See P. Langtofts chronicle by Robert of Brunne, p.* 304, *and the publishers glossary.*

Schende. *p.* 23. *ruin.*

Sehene. *p.* 20. *bright, shining.*

Schent. *p.* 5. *ruined.*

Schilterouns. *p.* 22. *See* Scheltron.

Schrewes. *p.* 41. *villains, wretches.*

Schrive. *p.* 46. *confess thyself.*

Scland. *p.* 11. *Zealand.*

Sembland. *p.* 30. *semblance, appearance.*

Sembled. *p.* 11. *assembled.*

Sen. *p.* 12. *since.*

Senin. *p.* 42. *after, afterward.*

Sere. *p.* 43. *several.*

Sergantes. *p.* 19. *sergeants*; *a sort of* gens d'armes, *according to* M. le Grand.

Skrith. *p.* 20.

Slake. *p.* 18. *asswage, quench.*

Slike. *p.* 2. *such.*

Slogh. *p.* 6. *slew.*

Smale. *p.* 1. *small.*

Snaper. *p.* 46.

Snell. *p.* 19. *keen, sharp.*

Socore. *p.* 1. *succour.*

Sone. *p.* 1. *soon.*

Sowed. *p.* 18.

Stalworthly. *p.* 15. *stoutly, vigorously, valiantly.*

Stareand. *p.* 10. *stareing.*

Stede. *p.* 3. *stead, horse.*

Stede. *p.* 9. *stead, place, room.*

Steren. *p.* 6. *stern, fierce.*

Sternes. *p.* 10. *stars.*

Stif. *p.* 16. *stout.*

Stile. *p.* 5. *a set of steps to pass out of one field into another.*

Stint. *p.* 19. *stoped, ended.*

Stirt. *p.* 49. *started, leaped, rushed, passed hastyly.*

Stound. *p.* 21. *space of time.*

Stowre. *p.* 5. *fight, battle.*

Strenkith. *p.* 25. *strengthen.*

Strenkith. *p.* 47. *strength.*

Strive. *p.* 19. *strife.*

Stroy. *p.* 10. *destroy.*

Suld. *p.* 4. *ſhould.*

Suth. *p.* 4. *ſooth, truth.*

Suth. *p.* 18. *ſooth, true.*

Swelt. *p.* 49. *dyed.*

Swink. *p.* 16. *labour,*

Swire. *p.* 37. *neck.*

Swith. *p.* 20. *quick.*

Taburns. *p.* 45. *tabors, drums.*

Tarettes. *p.* 11.

Tene. *p.* 20. *ſorrow, grief, trouble, affliction.*

Tha. *p.* 20. *the.*

Thareogayne. *p.* 9. *thereagainſt.*

Thir. *p.* 10. *theſe.*

Tho. *p.* 14. *thoſe.*

Tide. *p.* 4. *betid.*

Tight. *p.* 22.

Timber. *p.* 22. *deſtruction? The word occurs, as a verb, in the* Aunter of ſir Gawane: .

　　" *Thus ſhall a Tyber untrue* tymber *with tene.*"

Tint. *p.* 32. *loſt.*

Tithandes. *p.* 10. *tidings.*

To-dongyn. *p.* 32. *dung down, overthrown.*

Trais. *p.* 32. *betray.*

Traiſted. *p.* 15. *truſted.*

Treget. *p.* 31. *deceit, treachery, juggleing, impoſture.*

Treſt. *p.* 32. *truſt.*

Trew. *p.* 1. *true.*

Trey. *p.* 22. *a word nearly ſynonimous, perhaps, with* tene, *(which ſee,) and generally uſed in its company. See R. of Brunne, pp.* 235, 304; *and before, p.* 96.

Trone. *p. 1. throne.*

Trow. *p. 24. believe.*

Trus. *p. 50.*

Tyde. *p. 2. time.*

Tyll. *p. 1. to.*

Tyne. *p. 46. lofe.*

Umfet. *p. 30. befet; a contraction, perhaps, of* umbefet, *a word ufed by Wyntown :*

> *" And* wmbefet *the Scottis there."*

Umftride. *p. 16. beftride.*

Uncurtayfe. *p. 32. uncourteous.*

Unhale. *p. 24. unfound.*

Unkind. *p. 18. unnatural.*

Unfele. *p. 41.*

Wait. *p. 4.*

Wakkind. *p. 43. awakened.* Wakkins. *p. 22. awakens.*

Wald. *p. 2. would.*

Wall. *p. 21.*

Walld. *p. 15. would.*

Wane. *p. 11. quantity, plenty. Thus in* Ywayn *and* Gawin :

> *" Of maidens was thar fo* gude wane
> *That ilka knight myght tak ane."*

Waniand. *pp. 19, 41, 45. decreafe or wane of the moon ?*

Wapin. *p. 19. weapon.*

Wapind. *p. 14. weaponed, armed.*

Wappen, *p. 41. weapon.*

War. *p. 6. l. 6.*

Wede. *p. 19. apparel.*

Weder. *p. 15. weather.*

Wele. *p.* 3. well.—werldly wele. *p.* 8. *worldly wealth.*

Well. *p.* 19. *very.—p.* 31. *good fortune.*

Wen. *p.* 11. *go, or went. It should probably be* wend.

Wend. *p.* 4. *go.*

Wend. Wened. *p.* 10. *thought, suppofed, conjectured.*

Went. *p.* 22. *gone.*

Wepeand. *p.* 36. *weeping.*

Were. *p.* 2. *war.* Were men. *p.* 45. *men of war.*

Wery. *p.* 7. *curfe. So in the* Aunter of fir Gawane :
  " *But he fhal wring his honde and* warry *the wyle.*"

Wex. *p.* 12. *waxed, grew, became.*

Whilke. *p.* 9. *which, what.*

Whilum. *p.* 34. *fometime, formerly.*

Whore. *p.* 40. *where.*

Whote. *pp.* 4, 8. *woteft, knoweft.*

Wight. *p.* 16. *ftrong, ftout.*

Wikked. *p.* 49. *difficult?*

Wiltou. *p.* 7. *wilt thou.*

Win. *p.* 49. *take, get.*

Wit. *p.* 14. *informed?* Sent Edward to wit. *p.* 19. *fent to inform him, fent him information.*

Withowten. *p.* 8. *without.*

Witten. *p.* 26. *know.*

Wode. *p.* 25. *mad.*

Won. *p.* 7. *dwell.* Wonand. *p.* 25. *dwelling.*

Wonde. *p.* 40. *ftop, ftay.*

Wone. *p.* 14. *number, company.*

Wonen. *p.* 29. *won, got.*

Woning. *p.* 13. *dwelling, refidence, habitation.— p.* 48, *place.*

Wonnen. es wonnen. *p.* 19. *are won, are had as eafyly, or are as perfectly at mercy, as an unarmed man?—p.* 34. *won, got.*

Worthli. *p.* 19. Worthly. *p.* 45. *worthy.*

Wreke. *p.* 48. *revenge.* Wroken. *p.* 6. *revenged.*

Wrote. *p.* 33. *undermine, overthrow, properly to root up as fwine do:* wrotan, *Saxon.*

Wurthi. *p.* 21. *worthy.*

Zate. *p.* 38. *gate.—Note, this character* (Z), *at the begin- ing of a fyllable, had, uniformly, the power of* Y; *in the middle of one it had, ufually, that of* G H: *but it never oc- curs in the latter fituation throughout thefe poems.*

Zere. *p.* 12. *years.*

Zit. *p.* 19. *yet.*

Zolden. *p.* 37. *yielded, delivered up.*

Zong. *p.* 8. *young.*

Zow. *p.* 1. *you.*

Zow. *p.* 6. *your.*

CORRECTIONS

AND

ADDITIONAL NOTES.

P. 6. *l.* 13. Striflin] *Stirling.*

P. 7. Rughfute-riveling] *delete the hyphen, and place one between* Rugh *and* fute.

P. 11. *l.* 4. Armouth] *Yarmouth, in Norfolk.*

P. 18. *l.* 12. the Swin] *A river or passage between the ile of Cadsand and the S. W. continent of Flanders.*

———— *l.* 17. the Slufe] *or the Sluys (p.* 20) *a sea-port, belonging, at present, to the Dutch, opposite the ile of Cadsand, in what was then the county of Flanders.*

P. 19. *l.* 2. Arwell] *Orwell-haven in Suffolk.*

———— *l.* 9. Blankebergh] *Blankenberg, a sea-port, in the county of Flanders, between Ostend and the Sluys.*

P. 20. *l.* 20. Cagent] *the ile of Cadsand, in the mouth of the Scheld.*

P. 27. Hogges] *or* La Hogue, *a sea-port-town of Normandy, about two leagues S. of Barfleur.*

P. 28. *ll.* 6, 11. Thretty-thowsand] *delete the hyphen.*

P. 65. *l.* 18. *after* interview, *add:*

The moſt authentic account of this transaction is, probably, that given by Langtoft, or his translator, each of whom was living at the time :

> " Of William haf ze herd, how his endyng was,
> Now of kyng Robert to telle zow his trespas.
> Als Lenten tide com in, Cristen mans lauh,
> He sent for Jon Comyn, the lord of Badenauh ;
> To Dounfres suld he come, unto the Minours kirke,
> A spekyng ther thei nome, the Comyn wild not wirke,
> Ne do after the sawe of Roberd the Brus.
> Away he gan him drawe, his conseil to refus,
> Roberd with a knyve the Comyn ther he smote,
> Thorgh whilk wounde his lyve he loft, wele i wote.
> He zede to the hie autere, & stode & rested him thore,
> Com Roberdes squiere, & wonded him wele more,
> For he wild not consent, to reise no folie,
> Ne do als he ment, to gynne to mak partie,
> Ageyn kyng Edward, Scotland to dereyne,
> With werre & batail hard, reve him his demeyne."

P. 65. l. 26. Before Saint-Johnes-toune, *insert l. 7. and, after* Duplin, *add :*

Among all the English writers, historians or poets, perhaps the Scots have not a more inveterate enemy than Peter Langtoft, or his congenial translator, Robert Mannyng, who omits no opportunity of exercising his satyrical vein upon them. He even prays for their destruction, and wishes the whole country sunk to hell.

> " Jhesu so meke, i the biseke, on croice that was wonded,
> Grante me that bone, the Scottes sone alle be confonded !"

p. 283.

" Wales, wo the be, the fende the confound !
Scotland, whi ue mot i fe 'the' fonken to helle ground?
P. 265.

See alfo p. 279, and the prefent glosfary, under the word
RIVELING.

The Englifh, indeed, feem, in all ages, to have thought it
esfential to the character of a good patriot to hate and vilify
their neighbours; but it is not too late, one would hope, for
them to be taught better manners.

P. 81. *l.* 8. kyng Robert of Cicyle.] *Concerning this fage
and fcientific monarch, and of the pride which occafioned his
downfall, there is an old metrical romance, or legend, extant in
MS. Mister Warton, very ftrangely, fuppofes* Robert Cicyll
(*the title, he fays, of an old Englifh morality?*) *a corruption
of* Robert the devil.

P. 93. *l.* 2. *After the parenthefis, add* See alfo Spelmans
glosfary *voce* COGONES.

P. 96. *note. Another copy of Mannyngs work, according
to Tanner, is in the archiepifcopal library at Lambeth. Both
repofitories, however, are prefumed to be inacceffible to all but
thofe peculiarly favoured by right or intereft.*

P. 115. *l.* 4. *Infert this note:* Leland, out of *Scala chro-
nica,* tells us exprefsly that " This Charles, electid emperor,
fled at the batail of Crescy." (*Col.* i. 562.)

—*l.* 11. *The following note, alfo, fhould have been here inferted:*
Prince Edward, then a youth of 16, is commonly pretended
to have himfelf flain the king of Bohemia, and, in comme-
moration of that event, to have adopted the badge and motto
born on that day by his royal victim, and which have been

N

ever fince appropriated to the princes of Wales. (See Cam-
dens *Remains*, 1674. p. 451.) This anecdote is, neverthe-
thelefs, very questionable, and perhaps totally destitute of
foundation. The *oftrich-feathers*, at leaft, were certainly
the badge, not only of the black prince, but alfo of his two
brothers, John of Gaunt and Thomas of Woodftock, and continued to be the favourite distinction of the houfe of Lancaster till the time of Henry VI. and even much later, as appears by the feal of the old countefs of Richmond, mother
to Henry VII. They are likewife asfumed by Richard duke
of York, and his fon, afterward king Edward IV. (See
Sandfords *Genealogical history*, 1677.) Some perfon or other
may, probably, be able to clear up this matter; and, at the
fame time, to account, upon better authority than has yet
appeared, for the origin of the TWO ROSES, which make
fo confiderable a figure in Englifh history. Camden, it is
true, in page 452 of the above work, alledges, that " John
of Gaunt, duke of Lancaster, took a *red rofe* to his device,
(as it were by right of his firft wife, the heir of Lancaster,)
as Edmund of Langley, duke of York, took the *white rofe*;"
and, in the preceding page, he fays that " Edmund Crouch-
backe, firft earl of Lancaster, ufed a *red rofe*, wherewith his
tomb at Weftminfter is adorned :" but, upon a pretty accurate examination of all the feals, arms, badges, and mo-
numents, of the earls and dukes of Lancaster, publifhed by
Dugdale, Sandford, and others, it does not appear that any
one of them ever ufed a *rofe* for his device. On the contrary, as has been already noticed, the favourite cognizance
of John of Gaunt, and from him, it would feem, of the
houfe of Lancaster, was the *oftrich-feathers*; two of which

appear upon the duchy-feal to this day. The rofes, therefor, of earl Edmunds tomb may have been introduced merely by way of ornament, at the fancy of the artift. That the king of Bohemia ufed the device in question does not, perhaps, appear from any ancient or creditable authority.

Some of our beft historians (as Murimuth, Walfingham, and Knyghton) agree in ftating that the king of Majorca was alfo killed at this battle, which the authors of the *Univerfal history*, for the reafons there given, pronounce a falfehood. The authentic difpatches, likewife, preferved by Robert of Avesbury (p. 136), only mention "*le roi de Beaume*;" and the filence of our author, Minot, is a corroborative testimony.

P. 140. *Add to the note:* Wallis, in his *Natural history of Northumberland*, (ii. 416.) fays that Copeland, attended by only eight of his fervants, carried David off in triumph to the castle of *Roxbrough*, of which he was governor. It appears, however, that this identical castle (of which, it is likely enough, Copeland had been governor, (fee Lelands *Collec.* i. 558.) as he actually was afterward, (*Fœdera*, v. 760.) belonged, at that time, to the king of Scots. (See Ridpaths *Border-history*, 332, 335.) Some historians, it feems, relate that the king was conveyed to *Ogle-castle*, (*Ibi.* 338.) which is very probable, as it had been lately built, and fir Robert de Ogle, the then posfesfor, was prefent at the battle, (Wallis, ii. 551.) where, in fact, he had a principal command: and thus, Froisfart, confounding *Ogle* with *orgueil*, may have created his imaginary "*chastell-orgueilleux*." Copelands own refidence was, probably, at South-Copeland, by Wooller? and not at *Copeland-castle*, which, at that period, belonged to a different name. It appears, from an excerpt in Lelands *Itinerary*, (viii. 50, b.) that he attempted the capture of king David by the advice of Thomas Carre his ftandard-bearer.

THE END.

www.ingramcontent.com/pod-product-compliance
Lightning Source LLC
Chambersburg PA
CBHW030125030726

47498CB00007B/2552